Edgar Thurston

Coins Catalogue No.2 Roman, Indo-Portuguese, and Ceylon

Edgar Thurston

Coins Catalogue No.2 Roman, Indo-Portuguese, and Ceylon

ISBN/EAN: 9783337558628

Printed in Europe, USA, Canada, Australia, Japan

Cover: Foto ©Andreas Hilbeck / pixelio.de

More available books at **www.hansebooks.com**

MADRAS GOVERNMENT MUSEUM.

COINS.

CATALOGUE No. 2.

ROMAN, INDO-PORTUGUESE, AND CEYLON.

Second Edition, revised with additions.

. BY

EDGAR THURSTON,

SUPERINTENDENT, MADRAS GOVERNMENT MUSEUM.

MADRAS:
PRINTED BY THE SUPERINTENDENT, GOVERNMENT PRESS.

1894.

CONTENTS.

I.—ROMAN COINS.

ROMAN COINS.

" What ! A gold coin amid these jewelled treasures
  Why send me such a relic ? "—So you say.
" Good to enhance some antiquary's pleasures ;
  Stamped for dead people in a buried day ! "

True now, but look a little ! If one ponder
  The legend of this piece, its gold may shine
With lustre leaving dull the gems of wonder
  Which I did lay in those dear hands of thine.

An aureus of the Roman empire—See !

Edwin Arnold.

IN the first edition of the 'Catalogue of Roman, Indo-Portuguese, and Ceylon Coins (1888),' I included all the types of coins of the Roman Imperial Series which are contained in the Madras Museum collection, although the majority of the copper issues were doubtless not discovered in India. In the present edition I have included only the coins which have been discovered in Southern India.

The earliest notice, so far as I am aware, of the discovery of gold Roman coins (aurei) in the Madras Presidency, is contained in a letter from Mr. Alexander Davidson, formerly Governor of Madras, dated July 12, 1787,[1] who writes as follows :—" A peasant near Nelór, about 100 miles north-west of Madras, was ploughing on the side of a stony craggy hill; his plough was obstructed by some brickwork ; he dug and discovered the remains of a small Hindu temple, under which a little pot was found with Roman coins and medals of the second century. He sold them as old gold, and many no doubt were melted, but the Nawáb Amir-ul-Umará recovered upwards of thirty of them. This happened while I was Governor, and I had the choice of two out of the whole. I chose an Adrian and a Faustina. Some of the Trajans were in good preservation. Many of the coins could not have been in circulation; they were all of the purest gold, and many of them as fresh and beautiful as if they had come from the mint but yesterday ; some were much defaced and perforated, and had probably been worn as ornaments on the arm, and others pending from the neck."

In 1800 a pot was dug up at Poláchi in the Coimbatore district, containing a great many coins of Augustus and Tiberius, which were all of the same weight and value, each weighing 56 grains. Concerning these coins Buchanan says :[2] " One of the kinds is of Augustus. The legend round the head is CAESAR AVGVSTVS DIVI F PATER PATRIAE, that is, *Cæsar Augustus, Diri Filius, Pater Patriæ.* Above the reverse, representing two persons standing with two bucklers and spears placed between them, the legend is AVGVSTI F COS DESIG PRINC JVVENT, that is *Augusti Filio, Consule designato, principe juventutis.* Under the figures is written CAESARIA or *Cæsaria,* at some city of which name it has been struck. The other coin is of the same weight, and belongs to Tiberius. The legend round the head is TI CAESAR DIVI AVG F AVGVSTVS—*Tiberius*

---

[1] *Asiatic Researches,* 1790, vol. ii, p. 332.
[2] *Journey through Mysore, Canara and Malabar,* ed. ii, 1870, vol. ii, p. 31.

Cæsar Divi Augusti Filius Augustus. On the reverse, representing a person seated and holding a speer in one hand and a branch in the other, is the following legend:—PONTIF MAXIM, or Pontifex Maximus."

In 1806 the following five gold coins, all of different types, were found at Karur in the Coimbatore district, figured by Colonel Mackenzie, and described some years later by Sir Walter Elliot,[1] viz., " 1. ΛVOVSΓVS DIVI F., with a very curious and apparently undescribed reverse like a dog or sow, or some large quadruped with its nose to the ground and its tail over its back, below which in the exergue IMP. x ; 2. the common type of Tiberius as Pontifex Maximus ; 3. of Antonia, CONSTANTIÆ. AVGVSTAE. (Akerman, D.C.I., p. 148, No. 1) ; 4. two of Claudius, one CONSTANTIÆ AVOVSTI (Akerman, I. p. 155, No. 2), and the other S.P.Q.R.P.P. on. C.S. in an oak wreath."

In 1810 a pot full of well-preserved coins of Augustus and Tiberius was dug up at Poláchi, and seven years later a silver coin of Augustus was found in one of the old tombs called *Pandu Culis*, together with a number of irregular-shaped punch-marked Buddhist coins.[1]

Concerning finds of Roman coins in the Coimbatore district, Mr. R. Sewell says:[2] " It is evident that there was at one time a very considerable commerce between the inhabitants of this district and the Romans, for there have been numerous finds of Roman coins made here. Mr. Walhouse (Ind. Ant. v, 237) thinks that this was in great measure due to the beryl mine at Padiyúr in the Dhárápuram taluk, for the Romans set great store by the beryl, and Pliny declares that the best beryls come from India." On this subject the Rev. Henry Little writes:[3] " He (Mr. Walhouse) says that in the Kángyam taluk (near Dhárápuram) of the Coimbatore district, at a village called Padiyúr, there is an extensive dyke of crystalline porphyritic granite in the gneiss rock ; the dyke abounds with masses of quartz with large crystals of the same, as well as felspar, cleavelandite and garnete ; the crystals of cleavelandite are remarkably fine, and it often occurs in large masses, in the cavities of which the aqua marina is found in six-sided prisms. Mr. Walhouse gives an account of the enlargement of a well in 1798 and the discovery of these gems ; also of a systematic search made by a Mr. Heath in 1819–20, resulting in the securing of 2,196 stones, which weighed 120 pounds and were worth £1,200." He then adds "it is highly probable that most of the best aqua marines of the true sea-green color used in modern times in Europe come from this well, and some consideration will now be offered endeavouring to show the probability, at least, that its produce reached Europe in classical times and may have been the object of Roman barter . . . . . Pliny first conjectured what science has proved, that it is but a variety of emerald, and says especially of it (*Nat. Hist.*, bk. XXXVII, cap. V) ; the best beryle are those which have the greenness of pure sea water, and come from India, seldom found elsewhere. He also remarks that they are most lustrous when artificially polished hexagonally, not being aware that they occur in six-sided crystals. Now whence came the aqua marines known to Pliny, and on which the Greek and Roman engravers exercised their skill ? In modern times the gem, besides occurring in the Indian well,

[1] *Madras Journal of Literature and Science*, 1844, vol. xiii, p. 214.
[2] *Lists of the Antiquarian Remains in the Presidency of Madras*, 1881, vol. i, p. 214.
[3] *Madras Christian College Magazine*, December 1833, pp. 344–6.

has been found in America (North and South), in Siberia, and at a few places scattered over Europe, particularly at Limoges in France. America and Siberia may be excluded from the sources of ancient supply. The localities in Europe are in regions little known to the Romans, and unmentioned by Pliny, who had the best means of information. It is unknown in Ceylon. Its ancient origin seems therefore limited, as Pliny says it was, to India, and there it is only known to occur at the locality in Coimbatore described in this note, where moreover the gem is distinguished by the true sea-green color specified by Pliny; elsewhere it is bluish or muddy in tint. It must be added too that most of the finds of Roman coins have been within a radius of 30 miles of this well, and it has been stated to me that between that locality and the west coast there are plenty of Roman coins, both silver and gold, owned by cultivators who now and then dispose of one or two of them when they go to any distant place to a festival."

I have been informed by Mr. Henry Sullivan, and the fact is recorded by Mr. R. Sewell [6], that when his father, Mr. John Sullivan, was digging the foundations of a house on the hill to the south of the lake at Ootacamund, now called Bishopsdown, about the year 1827, he discovered a gold Roman coin, which passed into the possession of Sir Walter Elliot; and it is noted by Mr. Sewell that in the valley behind Bishopsdown and Fernhill, called by the natives Púnthat, are some ancient gold workings.

In 1838 an aureus of Trajan in fine preservation was picked up by a woman gathering sticks on the side of a stony hill near the village of Athiral in the Chitwail taluk of the Cuddapah district.

Obverse.—Head of Trajan. IMP. TRAIANO. AVG. GER. DAC. P.M. TR. P.

Reverse.—A soldier with a spear over his shoulder, marching to the right. COS. V. P.P. S.P.Q.R. OPTIMO. PRINC.

A solidus of Zeno was found in company with three or four of the pagodas, called animitti, from their bearing the impression of an elephant, and with several silver coins of the type figured by Prinsep as no. 9 of his Ceylon series,[7] at the foot of an insulated hill in the Tirumangalum taluk of the Madura district in May, 1839. The type of the Roman coin, which has been pierced to be worn as an ornament, bears the armed bust of the emperor, with D. N. ZENO. PERP. AVG. and the type of Victory holding a long cross. VICTORIA. AVG.G.G. θ. In the exergue CONOB.[8]

Still more recently, in June, 1840, a hoard of Roman aurei was discovered at the village of Darphal, about 15 miles from Sholapur. They were contained in a small earthen pot, and only eighteen were secured, chiefly of the reign of Severus, but a few also of Antoninus, Commodus, Lucius Verus, and Geta. Drawings of a few have been seen, and some of these prove to be rare types, such as Severus.

ADVENTVI. AVG. FELICISSIMO.
FELICITAS. SAECVLI.
PORTVNAE. REDVCI.
PROVIDENTIA. Medusa's head.

---

[6] Op. cit., vol. i, p. 226.
[7] Journ. As. Soc., Beng., 1837, vol. vi, p. 298, pl. 20.
[8] No. 1 of Akerman's Des. Cat., ii, p. 381.

One of the emperor on horseback spearing a lion appears to refer to a type of Commodus (Akerman, No. 99), but the legend is illegible in the drawing. There is also a specimen of Lucius Verus with the type of Æsculapius, and SALVTI. AVG. V. S.P.Q.R. TR. POT. III. COS. II.[9]

"In the month of May, 1842, after a heavy fall of rain, an earthen pot was discovered in a piece of waste land belonging to the village of Vellalur, about four miles to the east of the town of Coimbatore, which on examination was found to be filled with silver coins. When brought to the Collector, they were found to be Roman denarii, 522 in number, chiefly of the reigns of Augustus and Tiberius, with a few of Caligula and Claudius. The earthen vessel in which they had lain was like the common terra-cotta *lota* of the present time. It was broken to pieces in the scramble of the finders to possess themselves of its contents. Vellalur is not known to be remarkable as a place of importance either in ancient or modern times.

"Only eleven different types were found to occur in the large number of coins above mentioned.

1. *Obverse.*—Head of Augustus ......134 examples.
   CAES. AVGVSTVS. DIVI. F. PATER. PATRIAE.

   Reverse.—The Pontifical instruments, and two bucklers between the standing figures of Caius and Lucius.

   C. L. CAESARIS. AVGVSTI. F. COS. DESIG. PRINC. JVVENT..

2. Head of Augustus.... 1 example.
   AVGVSTVS. DIVI. F.
   Diana Venetrix.
   IMP. X.

3. Head of Tiberius....378 examples.
   TI. CAESAR. DIVI. AVG. F. AVGVSTVS.
   The emperor seated in a chair.
   PONTIF. MAXIM.

4. Head of Drusus senior....1 example.
   NERO. CLAVDIUS. DRVSVS. GERMANICUS. IMP.
   A triumphal arch; on the frieze, DE. GERMANIS.

5. Head of Germanicus (son of the above)........ 1 example.
   GERMANICUS. CAES. P.C. CAES. AVG. GERM.
   Head of Caligula.
   C. CAES. AVG. GERM. P.M. TR. POT. III. COS. II.

6. Head of Agrippina...... 1 example.
   AGRIPPINA. MAT. CAES. AVG. GERM.
   Head of Caligula.
   C. CAESAR. AVG. GERM. P.M. TR. POT.

7. Head of Caligula ...... 1 example.
   C. CAES. AVG. GERM. P.M. TR. POT.
   Radiated head between two stars.

8. Head of Claudius.... 1 example.
   TI. CLAVD. CAES. AVG. GERM. P.M. TR. P.
   Female seated.
   CONSTANTIAE. AVGVSTI.

9. Head of Claudius. . . . . 1 example.
   DIVVS. OLAVDIVS. AVGVSTVS.
   A carpentum drawn by four horses.
   In the exergue EX. S.C.

10. Head of Claudius. . . 2 examples.
    TI. CLAVD. CAESAR. AVG. P.M. TR. VI. IMP. XI.
    Victory pointing with a caduceus to a serpent.
    PACI. AVGVSTAE.

11. Head of Claudius. . . . 1 example.
    OLAVD. CAESAR. AVG. P.M. TR. POT. IMP. X.
    An oak wreath, within which. S.P.Q.R. P.P. OB. C.S."[10]

As regards the same find of coins Mr. M. J. Walhouse says : " This discovery took place just before I joined the district. I took casts of some of the coins, which by order of Government were sent to Madras—whether there melted in the mint or reserved in the museum I know not. The coins were doubtless all of well-known and edited types ; a short description may, however, be archæologically interesting. Of the 522, there were 134 bearing the head of Augustus with inscription CAES. AVGVSTVS. DIVI. F. PATER. PATRIAE, on the reverse a trophy of arms between two standing figures, and legend C.I. CAESARIS. AVGVSTI. F. COS. DESIG. PRINC. JVVENT; and 378 bore the head of Tiberius with inscription TI. CAESAR. DIVI. AVG. F. AVGVSTVS, on the reverse the emperor seated, with PONTIF. MAXIM. Of the remainder, two bore the head of Claudius and legend TI. CLAVD. CAESAR. AVG. PM. TR. VI. IMP. XI, on the reverse a winged figure pointing with a wand to a snake, and inscription PACI. AVGVSTAE ; another bore the head of Claudius with DIVVS. CLAVDIVS. AVGVSTVS, on the reverse a chariot drawn by four horses abreast, with letters EX. S. C. There were two other types of Claudius, one bearing on the reverse a female seated, the other a wreath enclosing letters ; and two coins of Caligula bearing the emperor's head, on the reverse of one a head surrounded with rays. A single example bore a head of Augustus with AVGVSTVS. DIVI. F. and on the reverse Diana carrying a spear, accompanied by a deer or hound, and legend IMP. X. Two remaining types were indistinct, one bearing a sort of arch."

In his *Remarks on some lately discovered Roman gold coins* (1851) Captain Drury says : [12] " A most interesting discovery of a large quantity of ancient Roman gold coins has lately been made in the neighbourhood of Cannanore on the Malabar coast, not only remarkable for the numbers found (amounting to some hundreds) but also for their wonderful state of preservation. Many appear almost as fresh as on the day they were struck—the outline of the figures is so sharp and distinct, and the inscriptions so clear and legible. With very few exceptions, they are all of gold, and of the age of Imperial Rome from Augustus downwards, several of them being coeval with the earliest days of the Christian era. From what we have been able to learn regarding their first appearance, it seems that a few were brought into the town of Calicut and offered for sale in the bazaar by some poor natives, who, naturally supposing from their shining appearance that

---

[10] *Madras Journal of Literature and Science*, 1844, vol. xiii, p. 212.
[11] *Indian Antiquities*, 1876, vol. v, p. 239, foot-note.
[12] *Journ. As. Soc., Beng.*, 1852, vol. xx, pp. 371-387.

they were worth perhaps some trifle, gladly bartered them away for a day's feed of rice. The coins, however, speedily found their way among those who were not long in estimating their real value, and the natives, finding that some importance was attached to the glittering metal, began to rise in their demands, and at length sold them for one, five, ten, and subsequently, for fourteen rupees the coin. The purity of the gold especially attracted the notice of the jewellers and the wealthier natives, who purchased them for the purpose of having them melted down for trinkets and ornaments, and many, it is to be regretted, have been irretrievably lost in this way. The secrecy at first so carefully maintained by the natives in respect to the spot whence they brought them rose in proportion to the eagerness with which the coins were brought up, and for a long time all endeavours proved fruitless in ascertaining the precise locality wherein they were found. It now appears that they were accidentally discovered in the search for gold dust by the gradual clearing away of the soil on the slope of a small hill in the neighbourhood of Kottayem, a village about ten miles to the eastward of Cannanore. A brass vessel was also found, in which many of the coins were deposited. For a length of time the numbers appear to have been very great, and it has been stated that no less than five cooly loads of gold coins were dug out of the same spot . . . . It is impossible to make any correct calculation as to the numbers which have actually been found, but it might be mentioned that about eighty or ninety have come into the possession of His Highness the Rája of Travancore, and a still greater quantity has been collected and preserved by General Cullen, Resident in Travancore, while even after the lapse of more than a year from their first discovery they are still procurable from the natives in the neighbourhood of Tellicherry and Calicut. The most numerous examples which occur are those of the reign of Tiberius, and next to that emperor, those of Nero. It is not a little remarkable that both among these aurei as well as among the denarii alluded to as discovered at Coimbatore, 1842, the examples of coins of the Emperor Tiberius should in both instances have been more frequent than any other, although this may in some manner be accounted for when we consider that the reign of Tiberius extended over a period of twenty-three years—a long time in comparison with that of the other emperors except Augustus."

Translation of a native letter, descriptive of the locality, and first discovery of the coins.

Tellicherry, December 16, 1850.

"Agreeably to my last note, I now beg to furnish you with the information of the discovery of gold coins here. About three years ago certain Syrians residing at Keelaloor Dashom in Palashy Amsham of the Cotiaoum taluk were in the habit of collecting gold from the bed of the river Vanienkudavoo (by taking the sand and sifting it), which was between Keelaloor Dashom and Vengador. One day, whilst they were engaged in digging the bed of the river, a number of gold coins were found in a part where there was a mixture of sand and mud. These were lying buried in the ground, but not in a vessel. A great quantity was taken, but nobody knows how many. Some suppose that these might have been buried here in bags, which have been destroyed. At a distance of ten koles east of this, there is a garden belonging ·to some low caste people who always reside there. During the hot season there is water to a man's depth, whilst in the monsoon there is depth equal to four or five men. The stream runs through one side of the dry bed of the river, whilst the other is so filled up with sand that it is like an island. Below this island on the other side there is another current resembling a small canal, which is the place whence the coins are taken. Certain Maplamars of Curvoye taluk, hearing of the discovery of gold at this canal, proceeded thither and tried to collect some, and it is said that they also got some coins. Although what these people got is not so much as taken formerly by others, nobody knows what was the exact quantity. About the year 964 (1788 A.D.) it is supposed that certain Gentoo inhabitants of Coorg or Mysore were in the habit of trading in these parts. This being the time of war, some wealthy merchants might have, from competent reasons, cast their gold coins into the river. There is no story of a wealthy man having ever resided in any of the adjacent villages."

DESCRIPTION OF THE COINS.

Augustus born 63 B.C., died 14 A.D.; reigned 58 years.

1. *Obverse*—AVOVSTVS. DIVI. F. Head of emperor.
   Reverse—IMP. XIII. Two figures, one seated.

2. *Obverse*—Head of emperor. No inscription.
   Reverse—CAESAR. AVOVS. Triumphal qoadriga.

3. *Obverse.*—AVOVSTVR DIVI. F. Head of emperor.
   Reverse.—AVOVS.; rest illegible. Equestrian figure galloping.

4. *Obverse.*—CAESAR. AVOVSTVS. DIVI. F. PATER. PATRIAE. Head of emperor.
   Reverse.—AVOVSTI. F. COS. DESIG. PRINC.

   JVVENT. L. CAESARIS. Two figures of Caius and Lucius; standing between them are two shields on the ground.

" The inscription on the reverse of this coin would run thus: *Caius et Lucius Cæsares, Augusti filii, Consules designati, principes jurentutis.* Caius and Lucius were the grandsons of Augustus, upon whom was bestowed the title of *principes jurentutis,* and it was subsequently conferred upon the probable successor to the throne when he first entered upon public life. Tacitus explains this when he says: " Nam genitos Agrippâ, Caium ac Lucium, in familiam Cæsarum induxerat; neo dum positâ puerili prœtextâ, *Principes jurentutis* appelari, destinari consules," &c.,—Tac. Ann., 1, 3. See also Suet. in Aug. Cap. 64 et seqq. The origin of the designation 'Pater Patriæ ' given to Augustus by universal consent is thus described by Suetonius (in Aug. Cap. 58). Valerius Messala leaving the Senate House, said ' bonum faustumque sit tibi, domuique tum, Cæsar Auguste. Senatus te consentiens oum populo Romano consalutat Patriæ Petrem.'

Tiberius born 42 B.C., died 38 A.D.; reigned 23 years.

5. *Obverse.*—TI. CAES. DIVI. AVO. F. AVOVSTVS. PONTIF. MAX. Head of emperor.
   Reverse.—Figure of Clemency; a spear in one hand and olive branch in the other.

6. *Obverse.*—TI. CAESAR. DIVI. AVG. F. AVGSVTVS. Head of emperor.
   Reverse.—DIVVS. AVGVST. DIVI F. Head of emperor surmounted with a star. The star was used as a symbol of the protection of heaven.

·Claudius born 10 B.C., died 54 A.D.; reigned 14 years.

7. *Obverse.*—DIVVS. CLAVDIVS AVGVSTVS. Head of emperor.
   Reverse.—EX. S.C. A triumphal quadriga.

8. *Obverse.*—TI. CLAVD. CAESAR. AVG. GERM. P.M. TRIB. POT. P.P. Head of emperor.
   Reverse.—AGRIPPINAE. AVGVSTAE. Head of Agrippina, representing a young female.

" The inscription on the obverse would run thus : ' Tiberius, Claudius Cæsar, Augustus, Germanicus, Pontifex Maximus, Tribunitiæ potestate, Pater Patriæ.' There were two celebrated persons bearing the name of Agrippina ; one was niece of Tiberius and mother of Caligula, the other was mother of Nero. The image on this coin is that of the former.

9. *Obverse.*—TI. CLAVD. CAESAR. AVG. P.M. TR. P. IV. Head of emperor.
   Reverse.—IM. : rest illegible. A bridge, and figure seated.

" May not this coin commemorate the building of the celebrated Claudian aqueduct, which bears the emperor's name to this day, and is yet in use at Rome, though partly in ruins ?

10. *Obverse.*—TI. CLAVD. CAESAR. AVG. P.M. TR. P. IV. Head of emperor.
    Reverse.—S.P.Q.R. P.P. OB. C.S. The former is enclosed in a wreath or garland.

" This would run : ' Tiberius, Claudius, Cæsar, Augustus, Pontifex Maximus, Tribunitiæ potestatis undecimo (anno), Imperator, Pater Patriæ, Consulatûs quinto (anno). Senatus, Populusque Romanus, Pater Patriæ, ob cives servatos.' The device of a civic crown is very frequently met with. This was usually bestowed upon those who had saved the life of a Roman citizen. The senate, in bestowing honors upon Augustus, decreed that a civic crown should be hung from the top of his house, and this honor having been assumed by the later emperors, a crown of oak leaves with *ob cives servatos* in the centre is often found on the reverse of coins in those Imperial times.

11. *Obverse.*—TI. CLAVD. CAESAR. AVG. GERM. P.M. TR. P. Head of emperor.
    Reverse.—EX. S.C. OB. C.S. Enclosed in wreath as above.

" Ex Senatus consulto " began to be invariably used on coins in the reign of Augustus. A few republican coins are found with the same initials.

12. *Obverse.*—TI. CLAVD. CAESAR. AVG. P.M. TR. P. VI. IMP. XI. Head of emperor.
    Reverse.—S.P.Q.R. P.P. OB. C.S. Encircled with wreath.

13. *Obverse.*—TI. CLAVD. CAESAR. AVG. P.M. TR. P.X. IMP. P.P. Head of emperor.
    Reverse.—PACI. AVGVSTAE. Winged figure of Victory.

14. *Obverse.*—TI. CLAVD. CAESAR. AVG. P.M. TR. P. Head of emperor.
    Reverse.—PRAETOR. RECEPT. Emblem of concord representing two figures joining hands.

15. *Obverse.*—TI. CLAVD. CAESAR. AVG. P.M. TR. P. VI. IMP. XI. Head of
emperor.[14]
Reverse.—na. BRITANN. Triumphal arch. Emperor mounted, with
trophies.[14]

" A most interesting coin representing the arch erected by a decree of
the Senate to the Emperor Claudius on the final subjugation of Britain.
It was in the year 43 A.D. that the Emperor Claudius sent over a large
force to conquer the island, which he subsequently joined himself,
Vespasian, afterwards emperor, being his second in command. This
triumphal arch no longer exists, and, were it not for the representation
of it on coins, we should have remained in ignorance of its ever having
been erected.

Caligula born 12 A.D., died 41 A.D.; reigned 3 years 10 months.

16. *Obverse.*—C. CAESAR. AVG. GERM. P.M. TR. POT. Head of emperor.
Reverse.—AGRIPPINAE. MAT. CAES. AVG. GERM. Head of Agrippina.
The name of Caligula never appears on his coins, and Caius is
always expressed by C.

The above coin was struck in honor of his mother, Agrippina.

17. *Obverse.*—C. CAESAR. AVG. PON. M. TR. POT. III. COS. III. Head of
emperor.
Reverse.—GERMANICVS. CAES. P.O. CAES. AVG. GERM. Head of Germanicus.

A coin struck in honor of his father, Germanicus.

Drusus born 38 B.C., died 8 B.C.

18. *Obverse.*—NERO. CLAVDIVS. DRVSVS. GERM AVGVSTVS. IMP. Head of
Drusus.
Reverse.—DE GERMAN. Triumphal arch, surmounted with equestrian
figure, commemorative of the victories of Drusus in Germany.

19. *Obverse.*—NERONI. CLAVDIO. DRVSO. GERM. COS. DESIGN. Head of the
young Drusus.
Reverse.—EQVESTER. ORDO. PRINCIPI. JVVENT.

" Drusus was made consul 9 B.C. The ' ordo equestris ' established
123 B.C. Those who were admitted into the equestrian order enjoyed
several privileges apart from the rest of the citizens, such as their
distinction of seats in public assemblies, &c.

Nero born 37 A.D., died 68 A.D.; reigned 14 years.

20. *Obverse.*—NERO. CAESAR. AVG. IMP. Head of emperor.
Reverse.—PONTIF. MAX. TR. POT. . . . . . . IV. P.P. EX S.C. Figure holding
a spear.

21. *Obverse.*—NERO. CAESAR. AVG. IMP. Head of emperor.
Reverse.—PONTIF. MAX. TR. P.X. COS. IV. P.P. EX. S.C. Armed warrior.

22. *Obverse.*—NERO. CAESAR. AVG. IMP. Head of emperor.
Reverse.—PONTIF. MAX. TR. POT. IV. P.P. EX. S.C. Encircled in wreath.

---

[14] Concerning this coin Sir Edwin Arnold says (*India revisited* 1886, p. 260):
" Among the curious treasures of the Madras Museum, which the Governor (Sir M. E.
Grant Duff) has greatly developed, is a golden coin of Claudius, the emperor, struck to
commemorate the conquest of Britain, and discovered in excavating a foundation near
Madras. What chapters of fancy might be written about this *aureus*, which thus
strangely links the past and present of England's history, and came, perhaps, to India in
the scrip of St. Thomas!"

23. *Obverse.*—NERO. CAESAR. AVG. IMP. Head of emperor.
   Reverse.—PONTIF. MAX. TR. P.V. COS. IV. P.P. EX. S.C. Armed warrior.
24. *Obverse.*—NERONI. CLAVD. DIVI. F. CAES. AVG OERM. IMP. TR. POT. EX. S.C. Encircled in wreath.
   Reverse.—AGRIPP. AVG. DIVI. CLAVD. NERONIS. CAES. MAT.; rest illegible. Two heads, male and female.
25. *Obverse.*—ANTONIA AVGVSTA. Head of Antonia.
   Reverse.—SACERDOS. DIVI. AVGVSTI. Two torches in upright position.

"Antonia, daughter of Marc Antony, was born 38 B.C. and was married to Drusus Nero. The inscription on the reverse of this coin may allude to the custom of priestesses (sacerdotes) or flamens being appointed after the deification of the emperors to superintend their worship at Rome and elsewhere.

Antoninus Pius born 86 A.D., died 161 A.D.; reigned 23 years.

26. *Obverse.*—ANTONINVS. PIUS. AVG. OERM. Head of emperor.
   Reverse.—P.M. TR. F. XVIII. COS. IV. F.P. A temple.

"This temple may perhaps bear some allusion to that decreed by the senate to Antoninus' wife, Faustina, after her death.

Additional.

27. *Obverse.*—CAESAR. AVGVSTVS. DIVI. F. PATER. PATRIAE. Head of emperor.
   Reverse.—TI. CAESAR. AVG. F. TR. POT. XV. Triumphal quadriga.
28. *Obverse.*—TI. CAESAR. DIVI. AVG. F. AVGVSTVS. Head of emperor.
   Reverse.—IMP. VII. TR. POT. XVII. Triumphal quadriga.
29. *Obverse.*—TI. CLAVD. CAESAR AVG. OERM. P.M. Head of emperor.
   Reverse.—CONSTANTIAE. AVGVSTAE. Female figure seated.

As regards the coins referred to above as being in the possession of the Rája of Travancore, these are described by Bishop Caldwell, who says:[15] "Of the coins described, all belong to the reigns of the first five Roman emperors.

"All are in good preservation with the exception of nos. 3 and 4, which are partially obliterated. A duplicate of no. 10 is also considerably worn. Several of the coins appear as fresh as if they had but recently issued from the mint. One cannot omit noticing the beauty of the design and execution apparent in several of them, particularly the heads of Antonia and Agrippina, and the distinct and striking individuality of all the heads.

"It would be very desirable to endeavour to collect and examine the whole of the coins discovered near Calicut (of which these are a portion, and) which are said to have numbered several hundreds, all gold coins, and all, it is supposed, Roman imperial aurei. If this could be done, the number of examples of each type could be ascertained, undescribed types might be discovered, and a conjecture could be formed *at* what time, or at least, *after* what time, the coins were concealed where they have been found. As far as appears at present, they *may* have been concealed about A.D. 70. If an opinion can be formed from the worn

---

[15] A description of Roman Imperial aurei found near Calicut on the Malabar coast, and now in the possession of His Highness the Rája of Travancore.—*Trevandrum Government Press*, 1851.

or fresh appearance of the coins, as compared with their earlier or later date, and the absence of all coins later than the reign of Nero, it would appear that they could not have remained in circulation after A.D. 70 and probably not so long.

"From the conquest of Egypt by the Romans about B.C. 30 till the decline of their power, Roman merchants traded extensively with India, and especially with the towns on the Malabar coast, to which they learned to sail direct with the monsoon from the ports of the Red Sea.

"Having few commodities that would be considered valuable in India to exchange for silks and muslins, gems and spices, ivory and steel, they were obliged to pay for the greater part of their purchases in specie. Roman coins were in consequence introduced into India so plentifully that they appear to have formed part of the ordinary currency of the country, and even the *name* of the Roman *Denarius* has survived to our own day in that of the Indian *Dinar*.

"The beauty of the Roman coins, as compared with those of the Hindu princes, contributed to their diffusion throughout all parts of India, and was, perhaps, the principal cause of their preservation. The ordinary Hindu coins were without hesitation broken up to be made into jewellery, but the Roman coins must have been considered by many as jewels in themselves [16], and carefully preserved accordingly.

"As the coins in question were discovered in the interior of the country (it is said in the bed of a river), it appears improbable that the persons who concealed them were themselves Roman merchants; but they may have been native agents of the Roman merchants, or persons extensively engaged in trade at the time the Romans maintained their intercourse with India.

"Money and valuables were concealed on emergencies of various kinds, but especially on the breaking out of war between two neighbouring princes. Only one or two persons would be acquainted with the place of concealment, and, if it happened that they were killed in the war, or through the continuance of hostilities unable to return to the place, their secret died with them, and it was reserved for well-diggers or miners, for the action of rain, or changes in the course of rivers, to bring the hidden wealth to light."

The following coins are described by Bishop Caldwell :—

No. I.—Coin of the Emperor Augustus.

Obverse.—AVGVSTVS. DIVI. F. Head of Augustus, crowned with laurel.
Reverse.—IMP. XI. Diana Venetrix; a figure of the goddess Diana, represented as a huntress.

No. II.—Coin of Drusus senior, step-son of Augustus.

Obverse.—NERO. CLAVDIVS. DRVSVS. GERMANICVS. IMP. Head of Drusus crowned with laurel.
Reverse.—DE. GERMANIS. A triumphal arch decked with military trophies, on which stands an equestrian figure of Drusus.

---

[16] I have seen an aureus on the neck of a cooly woman, who was carrying a portmanteau up the Shevaroy hill ghát. *Anct.*

3

No. III.—Coin of Caius, grandson and adopted heir of Augustus.

Obverse.—AVGVSTVS. DIVI. F. Head of Augustus, crowned with laurel.
Reverse.—C. CAESAR. AVGVSTI. F. An equestrian figure of Caius, the
horse at full speed ; infantry standards in the background.

No. IV.—Coin of Caius, referred to above, and his younger brother
     Lucius, grandsons and adopted heirs of Augustus.

Obverse.—CAESAR. AVGVSTVS. DIVI. F. PATER. PATRIAE. Head of Augustus, crowned with laurel.
Reverse.—Standing figures of Caius and Lucius, each holding a shield
and spear, with sacerdotal instruments in the background. Under
the figures, C.L. CAESARES ; over AVGVSTI F. COS. DESIG. PRIN. JVVENT.

No. V.—Coin of Tiberius.

Obverse.—TI. CAESAR. DIVI. AVG. F. AVGVSTVS. Head of Tiberius.
Reverse.—DIVI. F. DIVVS. AVGVST. Head of Augustus, surmounted with
a star.

No. VI.—Coin of Tiberius.

Obverse.—TI. CAESAR. DIVI. AVG. F. AVGVSTVS. Head of Tiberius.
Reverse.—PONTIF. MAXIM. A sitting figure of the emperor, holding in
one hand a staff, in the other a leafy branch.

No. VII.—Coin of Caligula.

Obverse.—C. CAESAR. AVG. GERM. P.M. TR. POT. Head of Caligula, with
laurel wreath.
Reverse.—GERMANICUS. CAES. P.C. CAES. AVG. GERM. Head of Germanicus,
son of Drusus and Antonia, and father of the Emperor Caligula.

No. VIII.—Coin of Antonia, wife of Drusus, grandmother of the
     Emperor Caligula, and mother of the Emperor Claudius.

Obverse.—ANTONIA AVGVSTA. Head of Antonia.
Reverse.—SACERDOS. DIVI. AVGVSTI. Two torches.

No. IX.—Coin of Antonia.

Obverse.—ANTONIA. AVGVSTA. Head of Antonia, crowned with a cereal
wreath.
Reverse.—CONSTANTIAE. AVGVSTI. A standing female figure, emblematic
of Constancy, leaning on a staff and holding a cornucopia.

No. X.—Coin of Claudius.

Obverse.—TI. CLAVD. CAESAR. AVG. P.M. TR. P. IIII. Head of Claudius,
crowned with laurel.
Reverse.—IMPER. RECEPT. A representation of the Prætorian camp at
Rome, on the tribunal of which is a sitting figure of the emperor.

No. XI [17].—Coin of Claudius.

Obverse.—TI. CLAVD. CAESAR. AVG. P.M. TR. P. IIII. Head of Claudius, crowned with laurel.
Reverse.—PACI. AVGVSTAE. A figure of Victory with a caduceus, before whom a serpent is retreating.

No. XII.—Coin of Claudius.

Obverse.—TI. CLAVD. CAESAR. AVG. P.M. TR. P. VI. IMP. XI. Head of Claudius, crowned with laurel.
Reverse.—CONSTANTIAE. AVGVSTI. A sitting female figure.

No. XIII [18].—Coin of Claudius.

Obverse.—TI. CLAVD. CAESAR. AVG. P.M. TR. P.X. IMP. P.P. Head of Claudius, crowned with laurel.
Reverse.—S.P.Q.R. P.P. OB. C.S. A wreath of oak leaves (the civic crown).

No. XIV [19].—Coin of Agrippina, wife of the Emperor Claudius.

Obverse.—AGRIPPINÆ. AVGVSTAE. Head of Agrippina.
Reverse.—TI. CLAVD. CAESAR. AVG. GERM. P.M. TRIB. POT. P.P. Head of Claudius, with the usual wreath.

No. XV.—Coin of Nero.

Obverse.—NERONI. CLAVDIO. DRVSO. GERM. COS. DESIGN. Youthful head of Nero.
Reverse.—EQESTER. ORDO. PRINCIPI. JVVENT. A shield.

No. XVI.—Coin of Nero.

Obverse.—NERO. CLAVD. CAES. DRVSVS. GERM. PRINC. JVVENT. Youthful head of Nero.
Reverse.—SACERD. COOPT. IN. OMNL CONL. SVPRANVM. EX. S.C. [20] The lituus, tripod, and other sacerdotal instruments.

No. XVII.—Coin of Claudius, struck after his death.

Obverse.—DIVVS. CLAVDIVS. AVGVSTVS. Head of Claudius.
Reverse.—EX. S.C. A carpentum drawn by four horses.

No. XVIII.—Coin of Nero and his mother, Agrippina.

Obverse.—NERO. CLAVD. DIVI. F. CAESAR. AVG. GERM. IMP. TR. P. COS. Heads of Nero and Agrippina.
Reverse.—AGRIPPA. AVG. DIVI. CLAVD. NERONIS. CAES. MATER. A car drawn by four elephants, in which are seated two soldiers, one of whom has his helmet elevated on the point of his spear.

---

[17] Another coin in the collection similar to this one, but of different mintage, has on the obverse TI. CLAVD. CAESAR AVG. P.M. TR. P.X. IMP. P.P.
[18] There are six coins in the collection similar to this, but varying from the XI XVI year of Tribunitian power.
[19] There is another coin similar to this in the collection, but struck apparently from different die.
[20] " Admitted as supernumerary priest into every college by decree of the Senate."

No. XIX.—Coin of Nero.

Obverse.—NERO. CAESAR. AVG. IMP. Head of Nero, without the usual laurel wreath.

Reverse.—A coreal wreath, within which EX. S.C.; round the margin PONTIF. MAX. TR. P. VI. COS. IIII. P.P.

No. XX [21].—Coin of Nero.

Obverse.—NERO. CAESAR. AVG. IMP. Head of Nero without a wreath.

Reverse.—PONTIF. MAX. TR. P. VII. P.P. COS. IIII. P.P. Figure of a Roman soldier, holding in his hands some kind of orb, surrounded with a flat rim.

No. XXI.—Coin of Nero.

Obverse.—NERO. CAESAR. AVG. IMP. Head of Nero without a wreath.

Reverse.—PONTIF. MAX. TR. P. VII. COS. IIII. P.P. Across the coin EX. S.C. A female figure resting on a long-jointed staff or spear-shaft, holding in her right hand three darts.

No. XXII.—Coin of Nero.

Obverse.—NERO. CAESAR. AVG. IMP. Head of Nero, without a wreath.

Reverse.—PONTIF. MAX. TR. P. VIII. COS. IIII. P.P. Across the coin EX. S.C. A standing figure of a soldier leaning on his spear.

"The next important discovery of gold coins," Dr. Bidie writes,[22] "took place in the Madura district in a piece of waste land near the village of Caliempootoor in the Iyempully taluk in the year 1856. [23] Two tank-diggers, while excavating brick-earth there, came upon an earthen pot, about the size of a mango, containing 63 coins of the Roman emperors. The pot was found about 1½ feet below the surface of the ground and near the bank of the river Shunmoogum Naddy, which is adjacent to the boundary of the Madura and Coimbatore districts. Before the authorities became aware of the discovery, 6 of the coins were made away with by the finders. The Government then directed that the whole of the remaining 57 should be purchased and sent to Madras, but only 28 were ultimately received, the remainder having been sold or lost in the Madura district. This is much to be regretted, as it is not improbable that, amongst those which were kept back, there may have been coins of dynasties not represented in the museum. The Madura coins form the chief portion of the Roman series in the museum." Concerning this series, Dr. Bidie writes further: [24] "The whole of the (gold) Roman coins in the museum belong to the

---

[21] There is a coin similar to this in the collection, but struck, apparently, when Trajane for the tenth time, and from an improved die.

[22] Catalogue of Coins in the Madras Museum, 1874.

[23] "About the same time three washerwomen of Karur, while searching for Fuller's earth, came upon a large chatty containing some hundreds, if not thousands, of *denarii*. There were five or six Madras measures of them. They were sold to Chetties for half their weight in rupees, and the finders have bought themselves land and built good houses with the proceeds. I cannot hear that a single *denarius* remained unmelted. My informant believes that most of them were like an Augustus I showed him."—The Rev. Henry Little, *Madras Christian College Magazine*, December 1883, p. 338.

[24] l. c.

Imperial series and extend from Drusus (B.C. 8) to Commodus, who ascended the throne 180 A.D. The following is a list of the emperors, etc., to whose reigns the coins belong :—

Drusus, senior			Domitian ..	81—96 A.D.
(consul) ..	— 8 B.C.		Nerva ..	96—98 „
Tiberius ..	14—37 A.D.		Trajan ..	98—117 „
Caligula ..	37—41 „		Hadrian ..	117—138 „
Claudius ..	41—54 „		Commodus ..	180—193 „
Nero ..	54—68 „			

" It will be observed that there are two breaks in the series, viz., from 68 to 81 A.D., and again from 138 to 180 A.D. On the whole, however, we have reason to be thankful for these rare and interesting records of the past, and it is quite within the range of possibility that the gaps may, in the course of time, be duly filled up by future finds of hidden treasure. As the collection stands even now, it looks so complete that one might almost suppose the coins had been carried to the East in the cabinet of some ancient coin collector, instead of having been introduced for purpose of commerce. It is to be regretted that there are no coins of the emperors who succeeded Commodus, and reigned until the upper empire ceased and the anarchy of the thirty tyrants began."

In 1878 a find of Roman coins was made near Karur in the Coimbatore district, concerning which the Rev. Henry Little writes as follows :—[13] "One afternoon last August (1882), while busy in my study, a native friend entered and placed on my table six small pieces of flat metal, almost round and a little larger than four-anna pieces, very black-looking, and much covered with earthy matter. To the inquiry what are these, an answer to the effect that they might be old Indian coins was returned, and then other matters were talked about. During this conversation one of the pieces of medal was rubbed quite mechanically a few times over the cloth on the table, and, when my eye next fell upon it, in silvery sheen and in somewhat antique Roman characters, there appeared to my astonished gaze the letters PONT.... ..MAX. I at once saw that the black lumps in my hand were Roman coins, and when they had been cleaned by acid and 'the image and superscription' brought out, there was no further room for doubt. I learnt that a soucar had about a hundred of these coins, and arrangements were made to obtain possession of them as expeditiously as possible. It seems they were dug up by a famine cooly in 1878 while engaged in deepening a water-course near Karur in the Coimbatore district, and that there were about 500 of them in an earthen pot. Two-thirds were melted to make bangles, and what fell to me was the remainder.

"My Roman coins are silver *denarii*, the New Testament *penny*. For five centuries after the founding of Rome, that is up to the third century B.C., the Romans had copper money only. In 269 B.C. silver coins were struck, and during the ascendency of Julius Cæsar a gold coinage was introduced, the commonest piece being the *aureus*, equal to 25 *denarii*. The weight of the *denarius* varied. In the time of Augustus 84 were struck for a Roman pound, making each coin to be about 60 grains. Several of those in my possession are about 58 grains in weight, showing that the lapse of time has told very little upon them, and with respect to other matters the same remark applies. The letters of the inscriptions are clear and the 'image' of the emperors is very bold and distinct, suggesting the inference that soon after they left the mint these coins were buried, and so suffered little loss by passing frequently from hand to hand.

"Twenty-seven of the coins belong to the reign of Augustus, and ninety to that of Tiberius. Although all the former commemorate the same event, they are not all from one die. On the obverse of those coins is a laureate head of Augustus, facing to the right, and beginning from the right-hand side of the bust the inscription runs as follows:—CAESAR. AVGVSTVS. DIVI. F. PATER. PATRIAE. On the reverse side stand two draped figures, each grasping a shield and spear which are grounded between them. Above the shields are a *lituus* or divining rod and a *simpulum* or small vessel for pouring libations of wine to the gods, which from its small size gave rise to the proverb *excitare fluctus in simpulo*, i.e., 'much ado about nothing.' Below the figure we read C. L. CAESARES., and following on from the right AVGVSTI, F. COS. DESIGN. PRINC. JVVENT.

"On the second coin we have a laureate head of Tiberius facing to the right with the following inscription:—TI. CAESAR. DIVI. AVG. F. AVGVSTVS. . . . . . On the reverse side of the coin we have a female figure seated on a chair of state. In her right hand is a spear, and the left holds a branch; the inscription is PONTIF. MAXIM., an abbreviation of Pontifex Maximus."

In 1889 [*] I received a letter from the Collector of the Kistna district, informing me that treasure, consisting of fifteen gold coins of the Roman Empire, had been found by a native, while he was digging in the old fort of Vinukonda, and that, as he concealed them instead of making them over to the nearest authority, they had become forfeit. The whole of this valuable treasure is now deposited in the Madras Museum, and consists of *aurei* of Tiberius, Vespasian, Domitian, Hadrian, Antoninus Pius, Faustina sen., Marcus Aurelius, Commodus, and Caracalla. One point of interest is that the majority are of types which have not been recorded in the previous finds in South India. Though many of the coins are bent, and some are perforated, as if they had been worn as ornaments, all are in a good state of preservation.

Vinukonda is reputed to be the spot where Ráma heard the news of the rape of his wife Sita, and the locality abounds with Hindu remains of great antiquity.

The following is a description of the coins:—

Tiberius.

1. *Obverse.*—TI. CAESAR. DIVI. AVG. F. AVGVSTVS. Laureate head of the emperor r.
   Reverse.—PONTIF. MAXIM. Vesta seated r., a spear in r. hand, branch in l.
2. The same as No. 1.

---

[*] This account is reprinted from my original note in the Journal of the Numismatic Society of London.

Vespasian.

3. *Obverse.*—VESPASIANVS. AVG .... Laureate head of the emperor r.
   Reverse.—A bull r., with head lowered and tail erect. In exergue
   [I]MP. XIII.

Domitian.

4. *Obverse.*—DOMITIANVS. AVGVSTVS. Laureate head of the emperor r.
   Reverse.—GERMANICVS .... Minerva r., with a shield on l. arm.
   raised to throw a spear.

Hadrian.

5. *Obverse.*—HAD ...... AVOVSTVS. Head of the emperor r.
   Reverse.—S. III. P.P. The emperor on horseback r., holding spear
   brought to the charge in r. hand.

6. *Obverse.*— ...... Laureate head of the emperor r.
   Reverse.—ADVENTV[I]. AVG. AFRICAE. Two figures secrificing at an
   altar.

7. *Obverse.*—ANTONINVS. AVG. PIVS. P.P. TR. P. XXII. Laureate head of
   the emperor r.
   Reverse.—VOTA. SOL. DECENN. II. The emperor veiled, standing l.
   over an altar, on which he is pouring a libation. In the exergue
   COS. III.

8. *Obverse.*—ANTONINVS. AVG. PIVS. P.P. TR. P. XIII. Head of the emperor r.
   Reverse.—LAETITIA. COS. IIII. Two female figures standing, one holding corn, the other a globe.

9. *Obverse.*—ANTONINVS. AVG. PIVS. P.P. TR. P. XVI. Laureate head of
   the emperor r.
   Reverse.—COS. IIII. Emperor standing l., holding in r. hand globe,
   and sceptre in l.

Faustina Senior.

10. *Obverse.*—DIVA. AV..... FAVSTINA. Head of the empress r., with
    hair braided.
    Reverse .... TAS. AVG. Female figure standing l. before an altar.

11. *Obverse.*—DIVA. AVGVSTA. FAVSTINA. Head of the empress r.
    Reverse.—AETERNITAS. Female figure standing, facing l., a globe in
    r. head, and sceptre in l.

Marcus Aurelius.

12. *Obverse.*—AVRELIVS. CAESAR. AVG. PII. FIL. Head of the emperor l.
    Reverse.—TR. POT. VI. COS. II. Minerva standing l., with Victory in
    her extended r. hand.

13. *Obverse.*—IMP. CAES .... EL. ANTONINVS. AVG. Head of the emperor r.
    Reverse.— ... CORDIAE. AVGVSTOR. TR. P. XVI. The emperor and
    Lucius Verus facing each other, with r. heads joined. In the
    exergue COS. III.

Commodus.

14. *Obverse.*—L. AEL. AVREL. COMM. AVG. P. FEL. Laureate head of the
    emperor.
    Reverse.—LIB. AVG. P.M. TR.[P.] XVII. COS. VII. P.P. Female figure
    (Liberty) standing l. with staff in l. hand, and cap of liberty in
    r. hand.

Caracalla.

15. *Obverse.*—ANTONINVS. PIVS. AVG. BRIT. Laureate head of the emperor r.
    Reverse.—SECVRITATI. PERPETVAE. Female figure seated on a throne, her r. arm supported on the back of the throne, and head resting on r. hand; sceptre in the l. hand.

In 1891* a find of silver Roman coins (*denarii*) was made in the village of Vellalur, in the Coimbatore district, by some natives, when taking out earth for a wall from some waste land. At the same village an earthen pot was discovered after a heavy fall of rain in 1842, which was found to contain 522 *denarii*, most of which were, as in the present instance, coins of the reigns of Augustus and Tiberius. The majority of the coins described in the present note belong to the same types as those which were found at Vellalur in 1842, and at Cannanore, and comprise issues of Augustus, Tiberius, Nero Drusus Antonia, Caligula, Claudius, Nero and Agrippina.

The following is a description of the coins:—

Augustus.

1. *Obverse.*—AVGVSTVS DIVI F. Laureate head of Augustus r.
   Reverse.—IMP. XIIII in the exergue. A Parthian or German presenting a child to the emperor seated on a curule chair.

                       1 specimen.

2. *Obverse.*—CAESAR AVGVSTVS DIVI F. PATER PATRIAE. Laureate head of Augustus r.
   Reverse.—AVGVSTI F COS. DESIG. PRINC. IVVENT. Caius and Lucius Caesar standing, each holding a shield and spear. C. L. CAESARES in the exergue.

                       188 specimens.

Tiberius.

3. *Obverse.*—TI. CAESAR DIVI AVG. F. AVGVSTVS. Laureate head of Tiberius r.
   Reverse.—PONTIF. MAXIM. Livia seated r, holding spear and branch.

                       328 specimens.

4. *Obverse.*— . . . . Laureate head of Tiberius r.
   Reverse.— . . . . . DIVVS AVG . . . . Head of Augustus r.

                       1 specimen.

Nero Drusus.

5. *Obverse.*—[NERO CLAVDIVS GERMANICVS IMP.] Laureate head of Drusus r.
   Reverse.—Equestrian statue on a triumphal arch between two trophies. DE GERM. on the frieze of the arch.

                       2 specimens.

---

* This account is reprinted from my original note in the Journal of the Numismatic Society of London.

6. *Obverse.*—NERO CLAVDIVS [GERMANICVS IMP]. Head of Drusus l.
   Reverse.—DE GERMAN[IS]. Trophy of arms.
   > 1 specimen.

Antonia.

7. *Obverse.*—ANTONIA AVOVSTA. Head of Antonia r.
   . *Reverse.*—[SAOERDOS] DIVI AVGVSTI. Two torches united by garland
   and bands.
   > 2 specimens.

Caligula and Augustus.

8. *Obverse.*—C. CAES. AVG. GERM. P.M. TR.P. Head of Caligula r.
   Reverse.—Head of Augustus, with radiate crown, r., between two
   stars.
   > 3 specimens.

Caligula and Agrippina.

9. *Obverse.*—C. CAESAR AVG. GERM. P.M. TR. POT. Laureate head of Caligula r.
   Reverse—AGRIPPINAE MAT. CAES. AVG. GERM. Head of Agrippina r.
   > 4 specimens.

Caligula and Germanicus.

10. *Obverse.*—C. CAESAR [AVG. GERM.] P.M. TR. POT. Laureate head of
    Caligula r.
    Reverse.—GERMANICVS. CAES. P.C. CAES. AVG. [GERM]. Head of
    Germanicus r.
    > 1 specimen.

Claudius.

11. *Obverse.*—TI. CLAV [D] CAESAR AVG. P.M. TR POT. ... Laureate
    head of Claudius r.
    Reverse.—Equestrian statue on a triumphal arch between two
    trophies. DE BRITANN. on the frieze of the arch.
    > 1 specimen.

12. *Obverse.*—TI. CLAVD. CAESAR AVG. P.M. TR. P. ... Laureate head
    of Claudius r.
    Reverse.—S.P. Q.R. P.P. OB. C.S. within a wreath.
    > 3 specimens.

13. *Obverse.*—TI. CLAVD. CAESAR AVG. ... Laureate head of Claudius r.
    Reverse.—EX S.C. OB. CIVES SERVATOS within a wreath.
    > 1 specimen.

14. *Obverse.*—TI. CLAVD. CAESAR AVG ... Laureate head of Claudius r.
    Reverse.—[PRAETOR. RECEPT.] Claudius giving his right hand to
    soldiers holding standard and shield.
    > 1 specimen.

4

15. *Obverse.*—[TI. CLAVD. CAESAR AVG. P.M. TR. P.] Laureate head of Claudius r.
    Reverse.—CONSTAN[TIAE AVGVSTI.] Female figure seated in chair.

                    1 specimen.

16. *Obverse.*—TI. CLAVD. CAESAR AVG. . . . . Laureate head of Claudius r.
    Reverse.—PACI AVGVSTAE. Victory pointing with caduceus to a serpent.

                    3 specimens.

17. *Obverse.*—DIVVS CLAVDIVS [AVGVSTVS]. Laureate head of Claudius I.
    Reverse.—[EX S.C.] *Carpentum* drawn by four horses.

                    2 specimens.

Claudius and Agrippina.

18. *Obverse.*—TI. CLAVD. CAESAR AVG. GERM. [P.M. TRIB. POT]. Laureate head of Claudius r.
    Reverse.—[AGRIPP]INAE AVGVSTAE. Head of Agrippina r.

                    2 specimens.

Nero.

19. *Obverse.*—[NERONI] CLAVDIO DRVSO GERM. [COS. DESIGN.] Head of young Nero r.
    Reverse.—EQVESTER ORDO PRINCIPI IVVENT. inscribed on a shield.

Nero and Agrippina.

20. *Obverse.*—NERO CLAVD. DIVI . . . Heads of Nero and Agrippina r.
    Reverse.—AGRIPPINA AVG. DIVI . . . . NERONIS. Car drawn by four elephants, in which are seated two soldiers, one of whom carries his helmet on the point of his spear, EX S.C. in field.

                    1 specimen.

"On the 17th April 1891, Mr. Maile, Railway Storekeeper, while superintending the construction of a site for store sidings of the new railway to Hindupur, between the Southern Mahratta Railway and the village of Yeswantpur, 3½ miles from the Bangalore City Station, in the Mysore Province, came across an earthen pot 1½ feet below ground, containing 163 Roman silver coins (denarii) in a good state of preservation, representing ten varieties, ranging in date between 23 B.C. to 51 A.D. This find, brought to light by the labourer's pickaxe, is believed to be the first within the territories of Mysore.

"It is difficult to conjecture how the coins were deposited in Mysore, unless they were brought there by some Persian horse dealers. A circumstance that gives rise to this supposition may be mentioned here, and that is that one of the coins bears the Persian word Karkh scratched on it. This is the name of a town in the west of Persia, which appears to have been built about the eighth century by Maruﬁ Karkhi, an eminent leader of the Suﬁ sect. The coin on which the word Karkh is scratched has the ﬁgure of a horse on the reverse, and the word is scratched beneath the ﬁgure of the horse, so that it may fairly be conjectured the word was scratched by a Persian as a means of identiﬁcation, and they may have been buried for safety in the troublous times that then existed, and it is probable that the owner may have died suddenly, or have been killed, without disclosing the secret of where his hoard lay hidden. It is also possible that the coins may have formed a portion of some loot, and have been hidden away, and the thief not able to go back to the place where he had deposited them."

"It is also possible that the coins may have been brought across the Indian Ocean by merchant traders direct from the Red Sea, as after Egypt had been conquered in the reign of Augustus, a navigator more venturesome than the others, struck boldly across the unknown expanse of waters, and reached the Malabar coast, thus opening the way for the despatch annually of a fleet of over one hundred vessels between the ports of the Red Sea and the Western Coast of India. The coins have been carefully and fully described by Mr. Lewis Rice, the Director of Archæological Researches in Mysore, and the following is a description of them:—

I. Augustus.

Obverse.—Legend AUGUSTUS. DIVI. F. Head of Augustus to right.
Reverse.—Bull charging to right with head down and tail over back. In the exergue Imp. x.
Obverse.—Head of Augustus to right, laureate. Legend CAESAR. AUGUSTUS. F. PATER. DIVI. PATRIA.
Reverse.—Caius and Lucius standing front, with spears and bucklers between them. Legend C. L. CAESARES. AUGUSTI F. COS. DESIG. PRINC. JUVENT.
Obverse.—Head of Augustus to right, laureate, with legend AUGUSTUS DIVI. F.
Reverse.—C. CAES. above horseman at full gallop, with infantry standards behind; below is AUG., the rest illegible. Beneath the horseman is scratched in Persian characters the word Karkh.
Obverse.—Head of AUGUSTUS to right, laureate. Legend CAESAR. AUGUSTUS. DIVI. F. PATER PATRIAE.
Reverse.—Head of TIBERIUS to right, with legend TI. CAESAR. AUG. F. TR. POT.

Antonia.

Obverse.—Head of ANTONIA with wreath to right. Legend ANTONIA AUGUSTA.
Reverse.—Two upright torches connected with a fillet, with legend SACERDOS. DIVI. AUGUSTI.

Tiberius.

Obverse.—Head of TIBERIUS laureate to right. Legend TI. CAESAR. DIVI. AUG. F.
Reverse.—Vesta seated on a square stool right, with spear in right hand and olive branch to left. Legend PONTIF. MAXIM.

Caligula.

Obverse.—Head of CALIGULA. laureate to right, with legend C. CAESAR AUG. GERM. P.M. TR. POT.

Reverse.—Head of AUGUSTUS laureate to right with legend DIVUS. AUG. PATER. PATRIAE.

Claudius.

Obverse.—Head of CLAUDIUS to right, with legend TI. CLAUD CAESAR. AUG. GERM. P.M. TR. POT.

Reverse.—EX. 8.O. OB. CIVES SERVATOS, within a wreath of oak leaves.

Obverse.—Head of CLAUDIUS, laureate to right, with legend TI. CLAVD CAESAR. AUG. GERM. P.M. TR. P.

Reverse.—Constancy seated to left with footstool, raising right hand. Legend CONSTANTIA AUGUSTI.

Obverse.—Head of CLAUDIUS, laureate to right, TI. CLAD. CAESAR. AUG. P.M. TR. P. VI. IMP. XI.

Reverse.—Winged female figure of Victory (?) standing to right, raising necklace with right hand, and holding out caduceus with left towards a serpent which is gliding away. Legend PACI. AUG.

As regards the discovery of Roman copper coins in Southern India, Mr. Sewell says: [26] " A number of coins of all ages have been found at the ' Seven Pagodas' (Mahabalipuram), amongst others, Roman, Chinese and Persian. A Roman coin damaged, but believed to be of Theodosius (A.D. 393), formed part of Colonel Mackenzie's collection." The reading given by Prinsep [27] of the latter coin, which was found at the Seven Pagodas together with several others bearing the same device, but of smaller size, ie:—

Obverse.—.... DOSIUS. P.P.... Head with star on the right.

Reverse—GLORIA. ROMANORUM. Three figures standing, armed with spears.

After describing [28] the finds of Roman gold coins as affording testimony of the frequent intercourse of Roman traders with the Indian Ocean, Sir Walter Elliot goes on to say: " Still more decisive proof is supplied by the existence of great numbers of Roman coins occurring with Chinese and Arabian pieces along the Coromandel coast. The Roman specimens are chiefly oboli, much effaced, but among them I have found the epigraphs of Valentinian, Theodosius, and Eudocia. These are found, after every high wind, not in one or two places, but at frequent intervals, indicating an extensive commerce between China and the Red Sea, of which the Coromandel coast seems to have been the emporium. The western traders must either have circumnavigated Ceylon or come through the Pámban passage, probably by the latter way, but in either case must have communicated freely with Ceylon." Farther, Sir Walter Elliot says elsewhere [29] on the same subject: " Along the Coromandel coast, from Nellore as far south as Cuddalore and Pondicherry, a class of thin copper die-struck coins, which, although not directly connected with the Andhra type, may be appropriately considered next. They are found in considerable numbers in or near dunes and sand-knolls in the vicinity of the kupams

---

[26] Op. cit., vol. i, p. 190.
[27] *Journ. As. Soc., Beng.*, 1832, vol. i, p. 406, pl. x, fig. 46.
[28] *Ind. Ant.* 1873, vol. ii, p. 242.
[29] *Numismal Orient.* Coins of Southern India, 1885, p. 35.

or fishing hamlets that stud the shore, together with Roman oboli, perforated Chinese coins, bits of lead and other metal, beads, fragments of charcoal, &c.

"These are collected by the wives and children of the fishermen after gales of wind or heavy rains, and purchased from them by the itinerant pedlars, called Labis and Morkayars, in exchange for useful necessaries, by whom they are sold to braziers and coppersmiths. The discovery of articles of this description in such localities indicates the existence of a considerable maritime trade in former times, probably during the first four or five centuries of the Christian era.

"The Roman coins are all of the smallest value, and are generally worn smooth, but on two or three the names of Valentinian and Eudocia have been read." It is much to be regretted that these coins are nearly always so worn that it is impossible to decipher their legend, and this is notably the case with the coins which are found, from time to time, in the Madura district. As regards this district, Mr. Sewell says: [30] "Mr. Scott, Pleader in the District Court of Madura, is in possession of a very fine collection of ancient coins, mostly found at Madura . . . . . The collection includes a large number of Roman copper coins (among which I noticed coins of Honorius and Arcadius), found in the bed of the river Vigai, as well as a Chinese coin from the same place. The discovery of so many *copper* coins of the Roman empire seems to argue the existence at Madura of a Roman colony at one period. If the coins were merely gold or silver, the discovery would not be so significant."

To the Rev. J. E. Tracy I am indebted for the following list of Roman coins in his cabinet, which were collected in the Madura district.

Aureus of Domitian.

Obverse.—Laureate head of emperor F. GERMANIC IMP. CAES. DOMITI. ANVS AUG.
Reverse.—Helmeted head of emperor F. P.M.T.R. POT. III. IMP. V. COS. X. P.P.

Aureus of Theodosius.

Obverse.—Head of emperor, with the legend of his names and titles.
Reverse. - Standing figures of the two sons of the emperor, and the legend SALVS. REIPVBLICAE. In the exergue CONOB.

Found in the Tirumangalam taluk.

Aureus of Constans II?

Found in the Tirumangalam taluk.

Copper coins of Theodosius, Honorius (?) and Anastasius, and several other copper Roman coins with indistinct legends from Madura.

Two Roman copper coins were sent in 1888 to the Madras Museum from Kilakarai, on the Madura coast, where they were found by Mr. J. P. James, Port officer, together with a large number of Buddhist, Chola, Pándyan, and other coins. Both coins are very much worn, and the legends on the obverse are entirely illegible. One bears on the obverse the head of some emperor, and on the reverse a cross

---

within a circle; while the other bears on the obverse the head of an emperor (Decentius or Julianus II?), and on the reverse VOT. XV. MULT. XX. in four lines within a laurel wreath fastened above with a circular ornament.

As regards the question how the Roman coins were originally brought to India, I may with advantage quote extracts from the article by Captain Drury[31] to which I have already referred. "We will now," he says, "consider, in a brief and somewhat imperfect sketch, to what extent and in what manner the Roman trade first arose and was subsequently carried on with the countries of the East, and more especially with that part of India, to which we would more exclusively refer, the Malabar coast, and also what degree of information the Romans actually possessed of this part of the country, and what kind of commodities were chiefly sought for their luxury or use.

"Previous to their conquest of Egypt, the Romans derived the benefits of Eastern commerce indirectly from the merchants of that country, who, under the reign of Alexander and the Ptolemies, monopolised the entire trade of India and the adjacent countries. Besides this route, the articles of Indian produce and manufacture were imported into Europe by a longer and more tedious way than that of the Red Sea. Being brought in vessels up the Persian Gulf and Euphrates, they were conveyed thence across land to Palmyra, then the grand emporium of Eastern commerce, and which, in its central position, became an important place from its flourishing and prosperous trade. From Palmyra the goods were carried to the different ports of Syria, and thence distributed to the various countries bordering on the Mediterranean Sea. At last the Romans, having subjected Greece and Syria to their sway and overcome the Republic of Carthage, made a descent upon Egypt, which soon yielded to the force of their arms, and from this time that rich and celebrated country was transformed into a Roman Province. This happened during the reign of Augustus, and about thirty years before the birth of Christ.

"From this time we may conclude that all direct intercourse of the Romans with the East commenced.[32]

"They followed up their victories with that characteristic energy for an increased trade which they ever displayed after the subjection of a

---

[31] *Journ. As. Soc.*, Beng., 1851, vol. xx, pp. 376-380.

[32] Dr. G. Oppert writes (*Madras Journal of Literature and Science*, 1879, vol. xxiv, pp. 209–210): "The more the commerce increased between India and the Roman Empire, the greater progress was also made in the art of navigation. The Western trade was viewed in India with favorable eyes, and the occasional embassies which were sent from India to Roman emperors show this fact plainly. Thus we hear of Indian envoys with precious presents being sent to Augustus, Claudius, Antoninus Pius, and Julianus.

"With respect to the knowledge concerning India, it is certain that the author of the Periplus (Maris Erythræi) did not double Cape Comorin, but Plinius was acquainted with the Koromandel Coast, and Ptolemy's knowledge embraced Burmah and even China. This country was visited by a Greek merchant Alexandros, who stopped at Kanton. Markianos of Heraklea and Ammianus Marcellinus provide on these points still more accurate accounts. We may, perhaps, be allowed to call Nanstathmos (Karaei), Theophila (Soradara) in Gujarat, Byzantium on the Malabar coast and other places Grecian colonies.

"As long as Rome was the sole capital of the empire, Indian goods went from Alexandria mainly to Rome; but when the empire became divided, Byzantium, or as it is now called Constantinopolis, participated in the receipt of the Eastern articles. Among the merchants who met in Alexandria, many Hindus were to be found, though the statue of the river-god Indus in that town was probably the gift of a Greek and not of a Hindu. The presence of Brahmans is even reported from Constantinople."

foreign people, and the glorious prospect of an undivided command of the Eastern trade added an unusual degree of vigour to their subsequent proceedings.

"Although the occupation of Egypt by the Romans offered them a far greater facility of communicating with India, yet their progress in this respect appears to have been slow and gradual, Augustus probably being more desirous of firmly establishing his authority in that country than extending his views to the conquest of remoter lands. No expedition to the countries bordering on the Red Sea appears to have been meditated till some seventy or eighty years after the Egyptian conquest. During all this time the trade had been carried on by Greek or Egyptian vessels. Without venturing far to sea, the commanders of these ships, starting from the port of Berenice (which still retains its ancient name), were in the habit of creeping slowly along the Arabian coast up the Persian Gulf, and never, perhaps, reaching farther than the mouths of the Indus, till at last a certain commander more venturesome than his predecessors, boldly pushed across the ocean, and, favored by the monsoon, safely reached the port of Musiris on the Malabar coast.[33] This successful voyage was but the prelude to other more fortunate enterprises, and so rapid became the increase of communication that not long afterwards a fleet of one hundred and twenty sail was annually wafted by the assistance of the monsoon from the Red Sea to the coast of Malabar, from which time a regular trade was established between the ports of Egypt and the Red Sea and those of the western coast of India.

"From the death of Augustus to the elevation of Trajan to the imperial throne, no important additions had been made to the limits of the empire with the exception of Britain. Trajan soon began to entertain the idea of carrying the Roman arms to the East, and, circumnavigating the coast of Arabia, vainly hoped at length to reach the shores of India; but the expedition was so far unsuccessful, and, the death of that emperor soon after taking place, the project was entirely abandoned by his successor Hadrian.

"The attempt of Trajan, who died 117 A.D., was never repeated by his successors, nor does there appear to have been any fresh acquisition made to the knowledge hitherto obtained of the western part of India until the reign of Justinian, when, owing to the increase of the silk trade, the rival power of the Persians sprang up. The empire was even then in its decline, and the traffic, and, consequently, the dominion over these seas being successfully disputed by a maritime people, the Romans were soon compelled to share, and finally to abandon, the profits of their commercial dealings with India, which had hitherto been crowned with such advantage and success.

"Even the information which the most celebrated writers of the first and second centuries had obtained of India was most inaccurate

[33] It is not exactly known where the present position of Musiris lies, or even of Barace, another port which was not far from it. Robertson, adopting the opinion of Major Rennell, is inclined to fix them both between the modern towns of Goa and Tellicherry, relying on a remark of Pliny that "they were not far distant from Cottonara, a country where pepper is produced in great abundance". In this case Barace might be Barcoor, as generally supposed, and Musiris in all probability Mangalore.

and imperfect, and Strabo, Ptolemy, Pliny, and others [34] equally ac-
knowledge and regret the scanty materials which they possessed regarding the true position and places of the Indian continent; yet Cape
Comorin was even then celebrated for its pearl-fisheries, and Ceylon,
discovered under the reign of the Emperor Claudius, had already sent
an embassy to Rome.

"It is most probable that the Romans never exerted themselves to
penetrate to any great distance for the commodities they procured from
the East, being contented to carry on their trade at those markets on the
Malabar coast which were easiest of access and sufficient for the purposes required. One or more ports, such as Musiris or Barace, were most
likely the chosen spots to which were gathered the necessary products
of the Indian countries from whatever side they were brought, and from
thence they were shipped to Egypt, and thence to the shores of Italy.
Merchandise was also conveyed, and, perhaps, still more frequently than
by sea, across the country, enriching several towns and cities on the
route which became the emporia of such commercial goods as were
despatched from the eastern to the western coast.

"Thus the modern town of Arambooly, called Arguropolis by the
Greeks, was celebrated in those days for its extent and for the busy
trade carried on there. Ptolemy also and Pliny mention Kotar or
Nagercoil under the names of Cottiara and Cottora metropolis; while
the Greek and Egyptian mariners, being afraid of doubling Cape
Comorin,[35] used to find a safe anchorage for their vessels in the little
harbours of Covalum and Colachull to the northern part of that cape,
and which were called in those days—the former Colis or Colias and
the latter Cojaci.

"The chief articles of export from India during the time of the
occupation of Egypt by the Romans were spices of various kinds,
diamonds and other precious stones, ivory, pearls, silk, &c., the latter
probably brought from China only. Cinnamon was perhaps more
extensively imported from Arabia or the eastern coast of Africa, in

---

"[34] The principal classical works which speak of India include—

Diodorus Siculus					circa	8 A.D.
Strabo	..	..	..	..	circa	23 „
Pliny	..	..	..	..	circa	77 „
Periplus Maris Erythræi		..	..	perhaps	81–96 „
Ptolemy	..	..	..	..	perhaps	138–181 „
Arrian	..	..	..	..	perhaps	150–160 „
Pausanias	..	..	..	..	perhaps	166–180 „
Bardesanes	..	..	..	..	circa	214 „
Ælian	..	..	..	..	circa	225 „

Dion Chrysostom and Plutarch (about 100 A.D.) also refer to India, and the Indian
embassies are described by Strabo, Suetonius, Dion Cassius, and Pliny; but with the exception, perhaps, of Pliny, the Roman historians seem to have had very little original information as to the far East." C. Reignier Conder, R.E., *Syrian Stone Lore*, 1888, p. 231.

[35] "It (Cape Comorin) is called Komaria Akron, Cape Komaria, by Ptolemy, and
Komarei or simply Komar by the author of the Periplus. The latter says: "After Bakare
occurs the mountain called Pyrrhos (or the Red) towards the south, near another district
of the country, called Paralia (where the pearl-fisheries are, which belong to king Pandion)
and a city of the name of Kolkhoi. In this tract the first place met with is called Balita,
which has a good harbour and a village on its shore. Next to this is another place
called Komar, where is the cape of the same name and a haven."—Bishop Caldwell's
History of Tinnevelly, 1881, p. 19.

Mr. Scott suggests that the Pyrrhos of the author of the Periplus is probably
Trichengode, "Teru sen kodo," the holy red point or mountain.

allusion to which a modern writer has remarked that the seaport of Aden was in those days used by the Romans as an entrepôt for the merchandise passing from India to Egypt. That seaport was apparently the same place which Ptolemy named 'Arabiæ emporium,' and the author of the Periplus tells us that a little before his time it was destroyed by the Romans; but it is to be presumed that the Romans followed up their victory by occupation, for the position assigned in the Periplus to Arabia Felix, together with the principle that it is nature which chiefly determines the site of a great maritime emporium, proves that the place in question was no other than Aden, which in the fifth century was the Roman emporium of the Indian trade." Pepper was entirely supplied from the Malabar coast, and large quantities were shipped every season for the markets at Rome, where it was esteemed one of the greatest luxuries of the day. When Alaric was besieging Rome in the fifth century and condescended to accept a ransom for the city, he expressly stipulated for the deliverance 'of 3,000 lb. of pepper,' so much value was attached to that commodity. All sorts of precious stones were eagerly sought after by the wealthier inhabitants, though it is singular that the Romans set a higher value on pearls than they did on diamonds. The former were procured as at the present day near Ceylon and Cape Comorin, and the mines at Sumbhalapura, in Bengal, are probably the same which yielded their treasures for the Roman merchants some twenty centuries ago. Lastly, ivory, ebony, and a few commodities of minor importance completed the list of useful or luxurious articles which were transmitted from this country.

"From the above brief sketch of the communication which the Romans had with the western coast of India and the enumeration of the chief articles of commerce, which attracted their merchants hither for the purposes of trade, we have little occasion to be surprised at the discovery of such coins as have from time to time been found in this country. The great difficulty lies in determining by whom and how they were actually brought here, and how many centuries may have passed away since they were either lost or deposited in those spots whence they are now taken. The oldest coins in the present collection are those of Augustus, and the latest those of Antoninus Pius, embracing a period of about one-hundred and forty years. We must, therefore, conclude that they were all brought here subsequent to, or during the reign of, the last-mentioned emperor, while the very remarkable state of preservation in which they exist would lead us to suppose that they had never been in extensive circulation or use previously. It can be no matter of surprise that no other memorials of those times are found upon this coast, such as buildings, &c., for the ancients obtained no footing in the country, but merely came and returned with their ships laden with merchandise.

"In the absence of all direct testimony as to the probable fact of these coins having been conveyed here by the Romo-Egyptian traders, there is another supposition, worthy of taking into consideration, whether they may not have been brought here by those Jewish refugees, who, emigrating from Palestine about the year 68 A.D., spread themselves over this part of the continent at that early period. That country was then a Roman province, and, consequently, Roman money was there in circulation. At that time ten thousand Jews with their families came and settled on the coast of Malabar, and dispersed themselves in various places, chiefly on the sea coast. Now, supposing several emigrations of the kind to have succeeded each other and taken place during the third and fourth centuries (Palestine did not cease to be a Roman province until the beginning of the seventh century), it is not unlikely that these coins may have been brought by them, and either from suffering persecution or oppression at the hands of the natives, they may have buried these treasures for greater security or concealment; but besides the Jews, the Nestorian Christians may have been instrumental in conveying foreign coins to these countries. In 485 A.D., they obtained a footing in Persia, whence they spread into almost every country of the East; but I do not consider this theory entitled to so much consideration from the fact of the coins being found in greater numbers on or near to the sea coast, on which account it would assuredly be more plausible to support the idea of their having been brought by the Romans from Egypt, or the Jews from Palestine, presuming the latter people in their emigration came either by way of the Red Sea or the Persian Gulf."

CATALOGUE

OF

ROMAN COINS IN THE MADRAS MUSEUM

FOUND IN SOUTHERN INDIA.

No.	Metal.	Obv.	Rev.
		AUGUSTUS.	
1	Ar.	CAESAR. AVOVSTVS. DIVI. F. PATER. PATRIAE. Laureate head of Augustus r.	AVOVSTI. F. COS. DESIO. PRINC IVVENT. Caius and Lucius Cæsar standing, each holding a spear. Above a *capeduncula* and *lituus* and buckler resting on the ground. C.L. CAESARES in the exergue.
2	,,	,,	,,
3	,,	,,	,,
4	,,	,,	,,
5	,,	CAESAR. AVOVSTVS. Head of Augustus r.	,,
6	,,	,,	,,
7	,,	AVOVSTVS. DIVI. F. Laureate head of Augustus r.	A Parthian or German presenting a child to the Emperor seated on a curule chair. IMP. XIII in the exergue.
		TIBERIUS.	
8	Au.	TI. CAESAR. DIVI. AVO. F. AVOVSTVS. Laureate head of Tiberius r.	PONTIF. MAXIM. Vesta seated r, a spear in r. hand, branch in l.
9	,,	,,	,,
10	,,	,,	,,

No.	Metal.	Obv.	Rev.
		TIBERIUS—*cont.*	
11	Au.	TI. CAESAR. DIVI. AVG. F. AVO-VSTVS. Laureate head of Tiberius r.	PONTIF. MAXIM. Vesta seated r, a spear in r. hand, branch in l.
12	Ar.	„	„
13	„	„	„
14	„	„	„
15	„	„	„
16	Au.	CAESAR. AVGVSTVS. DIVI. F. PATER. PATRIAE. Laureate head of Tiberius r.	TI. CAESAR . . . . . . A triumphal quadriga; horses walking r.
17	„	TI. CAESAR. DIVI. AVG. F. AVGVSTVS. Laureate head of Tiberius r.	DIVI. AVG . . . . . . DIVI. F. Laureate head r.
18	Ar.	. . . . Laureate head of Tiberius r.	. . . . . DIVVS. AVG. . . . . Head of Augustus r.
		NERO DRUSUS.	
19	Au.	NERO. CLAVD. CAES. DRVSVS. GERM . . . . . Head of Drusus l.	[SACERD]. COOPT. IN. OMN. CONL. SVP. NVM. In the centre the four instruments of sacrifice, viz., *simpulum*, *tripus*, *lituus*, and *patera*.
20	„	NERO. CLAVD. DRVSVS. GERM. PRINC. IVVENT. Head of Drusus l.	„
21	„	NERO. CLAVDIVS. DRVSVS, GER-MANICVS. IMP. Laureate head of Drusus l.	Triumphal arch surmounted by two human figures seated and an equestrian r. holding spear; horse prancing. Over the crown of the arch DE. . . . . .
22	„	. . . . DRVSVS. GERMANICVS. IMP. Laureate head of Drusus l.	Trophy, consisting of a standard, two shields crossed, and arrows. Round the margin, between the rays of the trophy DE. GERMANIS.

No.	Metal.	Obv.	Rev.
		NERO DRUSUS—cont.	
23	Ar.	[NERO. CLAVDIVS. OERMANICVS. IMP]. Laureate head of Drusus r.	Equestrian statue on a triumphal arch between two trophies. DE. OERM. on the frieze of the arch.
24	,,	,,	,,
25	,,	NERO. CLAVDIVS. [OERMANICVS. IMP.]. Head of Drusus l.	DE. OERMAN [IS]. Trophy of arms.
		ANTONIA.	
26	Au.	[ANTONIA]. AVOVSTA. Head of Antonia, crowned with a cereal wreath.	CONS [TANTIAE] AVOVSTI. A standing female figure, emblematic of Constancy, leaning on a staff and holding a cornucopia.
27	Ar.	ANTONIA. AVGVSTA. Head of Antonia r.	[SACERDOS]. DIVI. AVOVSTI. Two torches united by garland and bands.
28	,,	,,	,,
		CALIGULA AND AUGUSTUS.	
29	Ar.	C. CAES. AVO. OERM. P M. TR. P. Head of Caligula r.	Head of Augustus, with radiate crown, between two stars.
30	,,	,,	,,
31	,,	,,	,,
		CALIGULA AND AGRIPPINA.	
32	,,	C. CAESAR. AVG. OERM. P.M. TR. POT. Laureate head of Caligula r.	AGRIPPINAE. MAT. CAES. AVG. OERM. Head of Agrippina r.
33	,,	,,	,,
34	,,	,,	,,
35	,,	,,	,,

No.	Metal.	Obv.	Rev.
		CALIGULA AND GERMANICUS.	
36	Au.	C. CAESAR, [AVG. GERM.]. P.M. TR. POT. Laureate head of Caligula r.	GERMANICVS. CAES. P.C. CAES. AVG. GERM. Head of Germanicus r.
37	Ar.	„	„
		CLAUDIUS.	
38	Au.	TI. CLAVD. CAESAR. AVG. P.M. TR. P.X. IMP. P.P. Laureate head of Claudius r.	S.P.Q.R. P.P. O B. O.S. within a wreath (the *corona querces*).
39	Ar.	TI. CLAVD. CAESAR. AVG. P.M. TR. P. . . . Laureate head of Claudius r.	„
40	„	„	„
41	„	„	„
42	Au.	TI. CLAVD. CAESAR. AVG. P.M. TR. P. VI. IMP. XI. Laureate head of Claudius r.	Equestrian statue on a triumphal arch between two trophies. DE. BRITANN. on the frieze of the arch.
43	Ar.	TI. CLAVD. CAESAR. AVG. P.M. TR. P. . . . . Laureate head of Claudius r.	„
44	Au.	TI. CLAVD. CAESAR. AVG. P.M. TR. P.X. IMP. P. P. Laureate head of Claudius r.	PACI. AVGVSTAE. Victory pointing with caduceus to a serpent.
44·1	„	„	„
45	Ar.	TI. CLAVD. CAESAR. AVG. . . . . . Laureate head of Claudius r.	„
46	„	„	„
47	„	„	„
48	Au.	DIVVS. CLAVDIVS. AVGVSTVS. Laureate head of Claudius l.	*Carpentum* drawn by four horses. EX. S.C. in the exergue.
49	Ar.	„	„
50	„	„	„

No.	Metal.	Obv.	Rev.
		CLAUDIUS—*cont.*	
51	Ar.	TI. CLAVD. CAESAR. AVG. . . . . . Laureate head of Claudius r.	EX. S.C. OB. CIVES. SERVATOS. within a wreath (the *corona querces*).
52	,,	,,	[PRAETOR]. RECEPT. Claudius giving his right hand to soldiers holding standard and shield.
53	,,	. . . . Laureate head of Claudius r.	CONSTAN[TIAE]. AVGVSTI. Female figure seated.
		CLAUDIUS AND DRUSUS.	
54	Au.	TI. CLAVD. CAESAR. AVG. GERM. P.M. TR. . . . . Laureate head of Claudius r.	NERO. CLAVD. CAES. DRVSVS. GERM. PRINC. IVVENT. Head of Drusus l.
		CLAUDIUS AND AGRIPPINA.	
55	,,	TI. CLAVD. CAESAR. AVG. GERM. P.M. TRIB. POT. P.P. Laureate head of Claudius r.	AGRIPPINAE. AVOVSTAE. Head of Agrippina r.
56	Ar.	,,	,,
57	,,	,,	,,
		NERO.	
58	Au.	NERO. CAESAR. AVG. IMP. Head of Nero r.	PONTIF. MAX. TR. P. VII. COS. III. P.P. Draped figure of Ceres l. EX. S.C. in field.
59	,,	,,	,,
60	,,	,,	PONTIF. MAX. TR. . . . . EX. S.C. within a wreath (the *corona querosa*).
61	,,	,,	PONTIF. MAX. TR. P. II. P.P. EX. S.C. within a wreath.
61·1	,,	,,	,, but TR. P. VI. COS. IIII.

No.	Metal.	Obv.	Rev.

NERO—cont.

No.	Metal.	Obv.	Rev.
62	An.	NERO. CAESAR. AVG. IMP. Head of Nero r.	PONTIF. MAX. TR. P. VIII. COS. IIII. P.P. Figure r. with clothes descending to the knees; helmet on head; l. knee bent and supporting a globe (?) held in the hands. EX. a.o. in the field.
63	,,	,,	,,
64	,,	,,	,,
65	,,	,,	PONTIF. MAX..... A figure l, clothed; helmet on head, and wearing winged sandals; r. knee bent; foot resting on pedestal; r. hand holding quiver ; l. hand grasping spear.
66	Ar.	[NERONI]. CLAVDIO. DRVSO. GERM...... Head of young Nero r.	EQVESTER. ORDO. PRINCIPI. IVVENT. inscribed on a shield.

NERO AND AGRIPPINA.

No.	Metal.	Obv.	Rev.
67	,,	NERO. CLAVD. DIVI. ...... Heads of Nero and Agrippina r.	AGRIPPINA. AVG. DIVI....... NERONIS. Car drawn by four elephants, in which are seated two soldiers, one of whom carries his helmet on the end of his spear.

VESPASIAN.

No.	Metal.	Obv.	Rev.
68	An.	VESPASIANVS. AVG. .... Laureate head of Vespasian r.	Bull r, with head lowered and tail erect. IMP. XIII. in the exergue.

DOMITIAN.

No.	Metal.	Obv.	Rev.
69	,,	IMP. CAES. DOMITIANVS. AVG. P.M. Laureate head of Domitian r.	JVPITER. CONSERVATOR. Eagle on perch, with extended wings.
		,,	DOMIT. AVGVSTA. IMP. DOMIT. Head of Domitian; back hair in plaits and tied in long-looped knots; shoulders draped.

No.	Metal.	Obv.	Rev.

DOMITIAN—*cont.*

No.	Metal.	Obv.	Rev.
70	Au.	IMP. CAES. DOMIT. AVG. GERM. P.M .... Laureate head of Domitian r.	IMP. . . . . Seated nude figure of Jupiter.
71	,,	IMP. CAES. DOMITIANVS. AVG. P.M. Laureate head of Domitian r.	TR. POT. II. COS. VIII. DES. X. P.P. Standing figure of Domitian r., draped as Mars, with shield on l. arm, and throwing javelin with r. hand.
72	,,	IMP. CAES. DOMIT. AVG. GERM. P.M. TR. P.V. Laureate head of Domitian r.	IMP. XI. COS. XII. . . P.P. The emperor standing l., robed as Jupiter.
73	,,	DOMITIANVS. AVGVSTVS. GER- MANICVS. Laureate head of Domitian r.	COS. XIII. LVD. SÆC. FECIT. Salic priest standing l., with rod in r. hand and sacred shield on l. arm.
74	,,	DOMITIANVS. AVGVSTVS. Lau- reate head of Domitian r.	GERMANICVS . . . . . Minerva r. with shield on l. arm raised to throw a spear.

NERVA.

No.	Metal.	Obv.	Rev.
75	,,	IMP. NERVA. CAES. AVG. P.M. TR. POT. Laureate head of Nerva r.	COS. III. PATER. PATRIAE. A small vessel, a torch, a vase-like vessel, and the *lituus*.
75·1	,,	IMP. NERVA. CAES. AVG. P.M. TR. P. COS. II. P. P. Lau- reate head of Nerva r.	CONCORDIA EXERCITVVM. Two hands joined and holding a military ensign crowned with an eagle. The foot of the ensign rests on the prow of a vessel.

TRAJAN.

No.	Metal.	Obv.	Rev.
76	,,	IMP. TRAIANO. AVG. GER. DAC. P.M. TR. P. Laureate head of Trajan r.	COS. V. P.P. S.P.Q.R. OPTIMO. PRINO. A full length figure l., draped ; holding a palm leaf (?) in r. hand and spear in l.

No.	Metal	Obv.	Rev.

HADRIAN.

77	Au.	IMP. CAESAR. TRAIAN. HADRI-ANVS. AVG. Laureate head of Hadrian r.	COS. III. Draped figure l. holding ? in r. hand.
78	,,	HAD.... AVOVSTVS. Head of Hadrian r.	.. S. III. P.P. The emperor on horseback r. holding spear brought to the charge in r. hand.
79	,,	.... Laureate head of Hadrian r.	ADVENTVI. AVG. AFRICAE. The emperor clothed, in toga, with r. hand raised towards a female figure, with trunk of elephant on head, and sacrificing at a tripod.

ANTONINUS PIUS.

80	,,	ANTONINVS. AVG. PIVS. P.P. TR. P. XXII. Laureate head of Antoninus r.	VOTA. SOL. DECENN. II. The Emperor veiled, standing l. over an altar, on which he is pouring out a libation. COS. III in the exergue.
81	,,	ANTONINVS. AVG. PIVS. P.P. TR. P. XIII. Head of Antoninus r.	LAETITIA. COS. III. Two female figures standing, one holding corn, the other a globe.
82	,,	ANTONINVS. AVG. PIVS. P.P. TR. P. XVI. Laureate head of Antoninus r.	COS. III. Emperor standing l. holding in r. hand globe, and sceptre in l.

FAUSTINA SENIOR.

| 83 | ,, | DIVA. AV. .... FAVSTINA. Head of Faustina r. with hair braided. | .... TAS. AVG. Female figure standing l. before an altar. |
| 84 | ,, | DIVA. AVOVSTA. FAVSTINA. Head of Faustina r. | AETERNITAS. Female figure standing, facing l., holding patera and hasta. |

MARCUS AURELIUS.

| 85 | ,, | AVRELIVS. CAESAR. AVG. PII. FIL. Head of Aurelius l. | TR. POT. VI. COS. II. Minerva standing l. with victory in her extended r. hand. |

No.	Metal.	Obv.	Rev.
		MARCUS AURELIUS—*cont.*	
86	Au.	IMP. CAES. . . . . EL. ANTONI-NVS. AVG. Head of Aurelius l.	[CON] CORDIAE. AVOVSTOR. TR. P. XVI. The Emperor and Lucius Verus facing each other, with r. hands joined. COS. III. in the exergue.
		COMMODUS.	
87	"	L. AEL. AVREL. COMM. AVG. T.P. . . . . Laureate head of Commodus bearded r.	AV. III. . . . . II. Figure of Minerva (?) L holding spear in r. hand, and a small figure in l.
88	"	L. AEL. AVREL. COMM. AVG. P. FEL. Laureate head of Commodus r.	LIB. AVG. P.M. TR. P. XVII. COS. VII. P.P. Figure of liberty standing l. with staff in l. hand and cap of liberty in r. hand.
89	"	"	HERCVLI. ROMANO. AVG. Commodus as Hercules, standing naked l. having a club on his left arm, and a lion's skin pendent from the arm; his right hand is resting on a trophy of arms, which stands at the right of the field.
		CARACALLA.	
90	"	ANTONINVS. PIVS. AVG. BRIT. Laureate head of Caracalla r.	SECVRITATI. PERPETVAE. Female figure seated on a throne, r. arm supported on the back of the throne, and head resting on r. hand; sceptre in the l. hand.
		UNCERTAIN EMPERORS.	
91	Ae.	Head of emperor r.	A cross within a circle.
92	"	Head of emperor r.	Inscription VOT. XV. MVLT. XX. in four lines, within a laurel wreath, fastened above with a circular ornament.

SOME TYPES OF TITLES

ON THE

ROMAN COINS IN THE MADRAS MUSEUM.

Titles.	Remarks.
AVG. PII. FIL.	Augusti Pii Filius. On a gold coin of Marcus Aurelius.
BRIT.	Britannicus. On a gold coin of Caracalla.
COS. DESIG.	Consul designatus (Consul elect). On a silver coin of Augustus.
DAC.	Dacicus. On a gold coin of Trajan, who assumed the surname after his conquest of the Dacians.
DIVA. AVGVSTA.	On a gold coin of Faustina.
DIVI. AVG. F.	Divi Augusti Filius. On a gold coin of Tiberius.
DIVI. F.	Divi Filius.
DIVVS.	
GERMANICVS.	On a gold coin of Nero Drusus, who was styled Germanicus from his victories over the Germans. The surname was assumed by many of the subsequent emperors.(Caligula, Nero, etc.).
PATER. PATRIAE.	
P.C.	Proconsul. On a gold coin of Caligula and Germanicus.
P. FEL.	Pius Felix. On a gold coin of Commodus.
P M. TR POT. X. IMP. P.P.	Pontifex Maximus, Tribunitia Potestate x, Imperator, Pater Patriæ.
P.P.	Pater Patriæ.

Titles.	Remarks.
PONTIF. MAX.	Pontifex Maximus.
PONTIF. MAXIM.	„ „
PRAETOR. RECEPT.	Prœtorianis recoptis. On a gold coin of Claudius.
PRINC. IVVENT.	Princeps Juventutis. On a silver coin of Augustus, and gold coin of Nero Drusus.
SACERDOS. DIVI. AVGVSTI.	On a silver coin of Antonia.

SOME OF THE LEGENDS

ON THE

ROMAN COINS IN THE MADRAS MUSEUM.

Legends.	Remarks.
ADVENTVI. AVG. AFRICAE.	On a gold coin of Hadrian.
AETERNITAS.	On a gold coin of Faustina.
AGRIPPINAE. AVG.	On a gold coin of Claudius and Agrippina.
AGRIPPINAE. MAT. CAES.	Agrippinæ Matri Cæsaris. On a silver coin of Caligula and Agrippina.
C.L. CAESARES.	Caius et Lucius Cæsares. On a silver coin of Augustus.
CONCORDIA. EXERCITVVM.	On a gold coin of Nerva.
CONCORDIAE. AVGVSTOR.	On a gold coin of Marcus Aurelius.
CONSTANTIAE. AVGVSTI.	On gold coins of Autonia and Claudius.
DE. BRITANN.	On a gold coin of Claudius, struck in commemoration of the conquest of Great Britain.
DE. GERM.	On a silver coin of Nero Drusus. The legend refers to the victory over the Germans.
DE. GERMANIS.	On gold and silver coins of Nero Drusus.
EQVESTER. ORDO. PRINCIPI. IVVENT.	On a gold coin of Nero.
EX. S.C.	Ex Senatus Consulto. On gold coins of Claudius and Nero.
EX. S.C. OB. CIVES. SERVATOS.	On a gold coin of Claudius.
HERCVLI. ROMAN. AVG.	On a gold coin of Commodus.
JVPPITER. CONSERVATOR.	On a gold coin of Domitian.

Legends.	Remarks.
LAETITIA. COS. III.	On a gold coin of Antoninus Pius.
LIB. AVG.	Liberalitas Augusti. On a gold coin of Commodus.
LVD. SAEO. FEC. COS. XIII.	Ludos saeculares fecit Consul XIII. On a gold coin of Domitian.
OPTIMO. PRINC.	On a gold coin of Trajan.
PACI. AVGVSTAE.	On a gold coin of Claudius.
SACERD. COOPT. IN. OMN. CONL. SVPRA. NVM.	Sacerdos cooptatus in omni collegiâ supra numerum. On a gold coin of Nero Drusus.
SECVRITATI. PERPETVAE.	On a gold coin of Caracalla.
S.P.Q.R. OPTIMO. PRINC. COS. V. P.P.	On a gold coin of Trajan.
S.P.Q.R. P.P. OB. C.S.	On a gold coin of Claudius.
VOTA. SOL. DECENN.	Vota soluta decennalia. On a gold coin of Antoninus Pius.

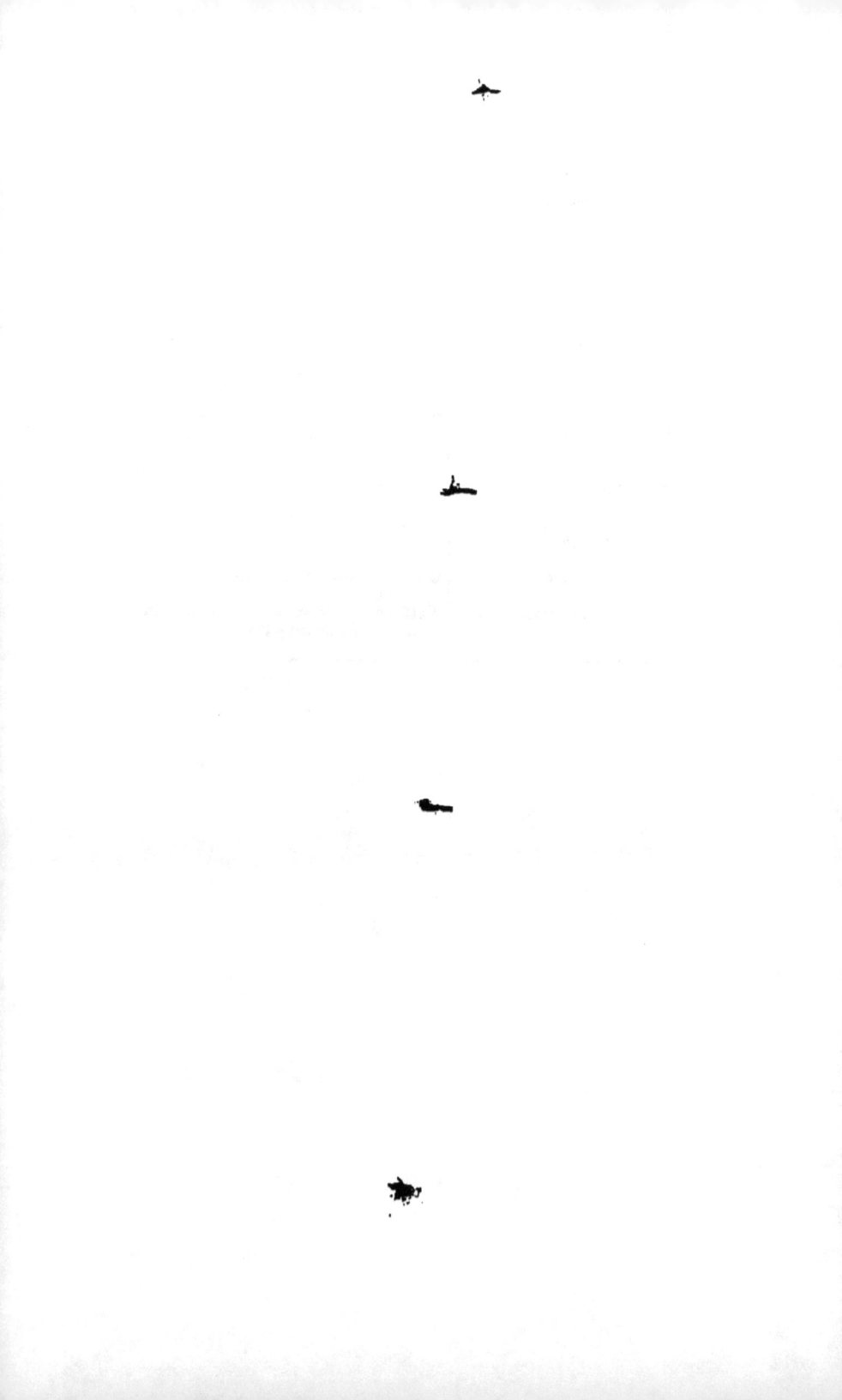

II.—INDO-PORTUGUESE COINS.

INDO-PORTUGUESE COINS.

THE history of the coinage for the Portuguese possessions in India, from the foundation of the Goa mint in 1510 by Afonso d'Alboquerque down to the present time, has been fully dealt with by Mr. J. Gerson Da Cunha in his admirable 'Contributions to the Study of Indo-Portuguese Numismatics,'[1] to which I would refer the reader who is interested in the subject, and to which I am indebted for the description of the coins.

The present catalogue contains only a description of the coins which are contained in the collection of the Madras Museum, and, to any one familiar with the history of the Indo-Portuguese coinage, it will be at once evident that the collection is very deficient in the coins struck prior to the latter half of the last century, and my efforts to improve it in this respect have proved fruitless; but this is not to be wondered at, for Mr. Da Cunha says : "The subject of the Portuguese coinage in India is involved in much obscurity. Money was first minted at Goa in 1510 A.D., only 370 years ago ; but its history is more vague and undefined than that of either the Greek or Roman coinage. The issue of coins by the viceroys, and often by the officers of the mint, without any intervention on the part of the viceroys or governors-general, was conducted in the most unsystematic, not to say capricious, fashion. The coins not seldom bore impresses, effigies, and legends, which had no connection whatever with the reigning monarchs of the period when they were issued. Some of them were still minted long after a new currency with crowned or profile busts of kings was introduced. Again, some of these latter were struck years after the kings whose busts they bore had ceased to live. These whimsical variations both in types and in the standard of money are in themselves enough to cause no little confusion in the study of Indo-Portuguese numismatics. But these difficulties are increased tenfold by an absolute want of examples of the early periods of the Portuguese rule in India, their place being but inefficiently supplied by some written reports and private memoirs. The coins of the xvith, xviith, and xviiith centuries are not only scarce, but even the written documents relating to them are rare or deficient."

Silver and copper coins struck in Portuguese India ceased to be legal tender in British India in 1893.

---

[1] Education Society's Press, Byculla, Bombay, 1880.

23601

ABBREVIATIONS.

Au. = Gold.   Ae. = Copper.
Ar. = Silver.   Br. = Brass.
Tg. = Tutenag.

CATALOGUE

OF

INDO-PORTUGUESE COINS IN THE MADRAS MUSEUM.

No.	Metal.	Obv.	Rev.
		KING D. JOAO V.	
		1706–1750.	
		RUPIA. 1748.	
1	Ar.	Bust of tho king r. with the legend JOANNES. V.R.P. The date 1748 in the exerguo.	Coat-of-arms of Portugal.
		KING D. JOSÉ I.	
		1760–1777.	
		MEIO PARDAO. 1753.	
2	,,	Bust of the king r. with the legend 10 ZEPII. IR.P. The date 1753 in the exorgue.	,,
		MEIA TANGA. 17xx.	
2·1	,,	Bust of the king r. The date 17xx io the exerguo.	Crown with 30 (tho value of tho coin in rcis) below. [Da Cunha, pl. VII, 7.]
		S. THOMÉ. 1766.	
3	Au.	Coat-of-arms of Portugal.	Cross of St. Thomas in the field, having at its upper angles 2—x, and the date 1766 in the lower ones.

No.	Metal.	Obv.	Rev.
		5 REIS. 1768.	
4	Ae.	Coat-of-arms of Portugal.	Cross of the Order of Christ, having in the angles the date 1768. [Da Cunha, pl. VII, 11.]
4·1	,,	,,	,,
		12 REIS. 1769.	
5	Tg.	Coat-of-arms of Portugal between the letters G—A.	The numeral XII with the date 1769 below it, all within a wreath. [Da Cunha, pl. VII, 10.]
		6 REIS. 1769.	
6	,,	,,	,, but numeral VI.
		4 REIS. 1769.	
7	,,	,,	,, but numeral IV.
		TANGA. 1774.	
8	Ae.	Coat-of-arms of Portugal.	TANGA in the field, surrounded by a laurel wreath, and having on the top a star. [Da Cunha, pl. VII, 8.]
		MEIO TANGA. 1774.	
9	,,	,,	G. between two stars in the field, having 30 R. above, and the date 1774 below: all encircled by a laurel crown. [Da Cunha, pl. VII, 9.]
		20 REIS. 1774.	
10	,,	,,	,, but 20 R.
11	,,	,,	,,
		10 REIS. 1774.	
12	,,	,,	,, but 10 R.

No.	Metal.	Obv.	Rev.
		PARDAO. 1776.	
13	Ar.	Bust of the king r: 1776 behind: PARDAO in front.	Coat-of-arms of Portugal.
		1777.	
13·1	Tg.	Coat-of-arms of Portugal.	Cross of Christ, and date 1777.
		RUPIA. 1777.	
14	Ar.	Bust of the king r: 1777 behind: RVPIA in front.	Coat-of-arms of Portugal. [DaCunha, pl. VII, 4.]

——

D. MARIA I.

1777–1799.

MEIO PARDAO. 1782.

15	,,	Laureate busts of the queen and her husband (D. Pedro III). r: OOA behind: 150 R in front: 1782 in exergue.	,,
		RUPIA. 1786.	
16	,,	Laureate busts of the queen and her husband: OOA behind: RVPIA in front: 1786 in exergue.	,,
		PARDAO. 1786.	
17	,,	Laureate busts of the queen and her husband: OOA behind: PARDAO in front: 1786 in exergue.	,,
		S. THOMÉ. 1792.	
18	Au.	Coat-of-arms of Portugal.	The cross of St. Thomee, having at its upper angles 12—x, and at its lower angles the date 1792.
		RUPIA. 1793.	
19	Ar.	Bust of the queen with widow's cap: OOA behind: RVPIA in front: 1793 in exergue.	Coat-of-arms of Portugal.

No.	Metal.	Obv.	Rev.

D. JOAO VI.

REGENT FROM 1799–1818.
KING FROM 1818–1826.

No.	Metal.	Obv.	Rev.
19·1	Tg.	Cross of Christ, and date 1799.	Coat-of-arms of Portugal, and letters D—D. (Diu).

RUPIA. 1813.

| 20 | Ar. | Bust of the regent laureate r. | Coat-of-arms of Portugal. |

PARDAO. 1818.

| 21 | ,, | Bust of the King laureate r: ooa behind: PARDAO in front: 1818 in exergue. | ,, |

PARDAO. 1820.

| 22 | ,, | ,, but 1820. | Coat-of-arms of the United Kingdom (i.e., the arms of Portugal with the sphere of Brazil). |

D. PEDRO IV.

1826–1828.

TANGA.

| 23 | Br. | Coat-of-arms of Portugal. | AP. (Asia Portuguese), within a laurel wreath, and т. below it. [Da Cunha, pl. VIII, 9.] |
| 24 | ,, | ,, | ,, |

MEIO TANGA.

| 25 | ,, | ,, | ,, with the addition of ½ between the letters AP. and т. |
| 26 | ,, | ,, | ,, |

RUPIA. 1828.

| 27 | Ar. | Bust of the king r: ooa behind: RVPIA in front: 1828 in exergue. | Coat-of-arms of the United Kingdom. |

No.	Metal	Obv.	Rev.
		1828.	
27–1	Tg.	Coat-of-arms of Portugal and letters D.D. (Diu).	Cross of Christ, and date 1828.

D. MARIA II.[1]

1834–1853.

RUPEE. 1833.

No.	Metal	Obv.	Rev.
28	Ar.	„ but 1833.	„

PARDAO. 1833.

| 29 | „ | Bust of Pedro IV. laureato r : GOA behind : PARDAO in front : 1833 in exergue. | „ |

PARDAO. 1839.

| 30 | „ | Bust of tho queen l. and legend PARDAO. DE. GOA. 1839 in exergue. | Coat-of-arms of Portugal surrounded by a laurel wreath. |

RUPIA. 1840.

| 31 | „ | Bust of the queen l. and legend RVPIA. DE. GOA. 1840 in exergue. | „ |

TANGA. 1840.

| 32 | Ae. | Coat-of-arms of Portugal between two laurel branches : 1840 in exergue. | 60 R. within a laurel wreath. [Da Cunha, pl. IX, 1.] |
| 33 | „ | „ | „ |

MEIA TANGA. 1840.

| 34 | „ | „ | „ but 30 R. |
| 35 | „ | „ | „ |

[1] " This distinguished prince (D. Pedro IV) abdicated the crown on behalf of his daughter, D. Maria, on the 2nd of May 1826, which abdication was ratified on the 2nd of March 1828. He then declared himself regent of the kingdom on the 3rd of March 1832." Da Cunha, *Indo-Portuguese Numismatics*, Bombay, 1880.

8

No.	Metal.	Obv.	Rev.

15 Reis. 1843.

No.	Metal.	Obv.	Rev.
86	Ae.	Coat-of-arms of Portugal within flowery embellishments : 1843 in exergue.	15 R—D. within a beaded circle.

Rupia. 1845.

37	Ar.	Bust of the queen diademed l. and legend MARIA II. PORTUG. ET. ALGARB. REGINA : 1845 in exergue.	Rupia. within a laurel wreath.
			[Da Cunha, pl. IX, 2].

Pardao. 1845.

38	,,	,,	Pardao. within a laurel wreath.

10 Reis. 1845.

39	Ae.	Coat-of-arms of Portugal : 1845 in exergue.	10 R.
40	,,	,,	,,

7½ Reis. 1845.

41	,,	,,	7½ R.

6 Reis. 1845.

42	,,	,,	6 R.

4½ Reis. 1845.

43	,,	,,	4½ R.

Pardao. 1846.

44	Ar.	Bust of the queen diademed l. and legend MARIA II. PORTUG. ET ALGARB. REGINA : 1846 in exergue.	Pardao. within a laurel wreath.

No.	Metal	Obv.	Rev.
		MEIO PARDAO. 1846.	
45	Ar.	Bust of the queen diademed l. and legend MARIA II. POR-TUO. ET ALGARB. REOINA: 1846 in exergue.	MEIO r. within a laurel wreath.
		6 REIS. 1848.	
46	Ae.	Coat-of-arms of Portugal: 1848 in exergue.	6 R.
		3 REIS. 1848.	
47	„	„	3 R.
		RUPIA. 1850.	
48	Ar.	Bust of the queen diademed l. and legend MARIA II. POR-TUO. ET ALGARB. REOINA: 1850 in exergue.	Coat-of-arms of Portugal: RUPIA DE OOA in exergue.
49	„	„	„
		PARDAO. 1851.	
50	„	„ but date 1851.	Coat-of-arms of Portugal: PARDAO DE OOA in exergue.
		100 REIS. 1853.	
51	„	„ but date 1853.	100 REIS within a laurel wreath.

D. PEDRO V.

1853—1865.

MEIO TANGA. 1861.

No.	Metal	Obv.	Rev.
52	Ao.	Coat-of-arms of Portugal within two laurel branches: 1854 in exergue.	30 R. within a laurel wreath.
53	„	„	„

No.	Metal.	Obv.	Rev.
		RUPIA. 1856.	
54	Ar.	Head of the young king r. and legend PETRUS V. PORTUG. ET ALGARB. REX : 1856 in exergue.	RUPIA. GOA. within a laurel wreath. [Da Cunha, pl. ix, a.]
		RUPEE. 1857.	
55	,,	,, but date 1857.	,,
		PARDAO. 1857.	
56	,,	,,	PARDAU. GOA. within a laurel wreath.
		MEIO PARDAO. 1857.	
57	,,	,,	MEIO. r. within a laurel wreath.
		PARDAO. 1860.	
58	,,	,, but date 1860.	PARDAU. GOA. within a laurel wreath.

D. LUIZ 1.
1861—1889.
PARDAO. 1868.

No.	Metal.	Obv.	Rev.
59	,,	Bust of the young king l. and legend LUDOVICUS I. PORTUG. ET ALGARB. REX : 1868 in exergue.	,,
		RUPIA. 1869.	
60	,,	,, but 1869.	RUPIA GOA. within a laurel wreath. [Da Cunha, pl. ix,].

No.	Metal.	Obv.	Rev.
		TANGA. 1871.	
61	Æ.	Coat-of-arms of Portugal and legend INDIA PORTUG: 1871 in oxergue.	TANGA 60 REIS. within a laurel wreath. [Da Cunha, pl. ix, 9.]
62	,,	,,	,,
		MEIO TANGA. 1871.	
63	,,	,,	½ TANGA 30 REIS. within a laurel wreath.
64	,,	,,	,,
		QUARTER TANGA. 1871.	
65	,,	,,	¼ TANGA 15 REIS. within a laurel wreath.
66	,,	,,	,,
		10 REIS. 1871.	
67	,,	,,	10 REIS. within a laurel wreath.
68	,,	,,	,,
		5 REIS. 1871.	
69	,,	,,	,, but 5 REIS.
		3 REIS. 1871.	
70	,,	,,	,, but 3 REIS.

No.	Metal.	Obv.	Rev.
		RUPIA. 1881.	
71	Ar.	Bust of the king r. and legend LUDOVICUS I. PORTUG. ET. ALGARB. REX: 1881 in exergue.	Coat-of-arms of Portugal with laurel branches, and legend INDIA PORTUGUEZA UMA RUPIA. [Da Cunha, pl. ix, 11.]
		MEIA RUPIA. 1881.	
72	,,	,,	,, but MEIA RUPIA.
73	,,	,,	,,
		QUARTO DE RUPIA. 1881.	
74	,,	,,	,, but QUARTO DE RUPIA.
		OCTAVO DE RUPIA. 1881.	
75	,,	,,	,, but OCTAVO DE RUPIA.
		QUARTO DE TANGA. 1881.	
76	Ae.	,,	Crown, and legend INDIA PORTUGUEZA QUARTO DE TANGA. [Da Cunha, pl. ix, 10.]
77	,,	,,	,,
		RUPIA. 1882.	
78	Ar.	Bust of the king l. and legend LUDOVICUS I. PORTUG. ET ALGARB. REX: 1882 in exergue.	Coat-of-arms of Portugal with laurel branches, and legend INDIA PORTUGUEZA UMA RUPIA.

III.—CEYLON COINS.

CEYLON COINS.

THE coinage of the island of Ceylon, both ancient and modern, has been already fully dealt with in the Numismata Orientalia [1] by Mr. T. W. Rhys Davids, who gives the following list of the kings of Ceylon from 1153-1296 A.D., those whose coins are extant being indicated by a star :—

1. Parákrama Báhu, 1153.*
2. Vijaya Báhu 11, 1186, nephew of the last.
3. Niṣṣanka Malla,* 1187, a prince of Kalinga.
4. Wikrama Báhu 11, 1196, brother of Niṣṣanka Malla.
5. Coḍaganga,* 1196, nephew of Niṣṣanka Malla.
6. Líláwatí (queen),* 1197, widow of Parákrama Báhu.
7. Sáhasa Malla,* 1200, brother (?) of Niṣṣanka Malla.
8. Kalyánawati (queen), 1202, widow of Niṣṣanka Malla.
9. Dharmáoka,* 1208.
10. Líláwatí (restored), 1209.
11. Pándi Parákrama Báhu 1211, Malabar usurper.
12. Mágha 1214, a Kálingan prince.
13. Dambadeniya Wijaya Báhu, 1235, founder of a new dynasty.
14. Dambadeniya Parákrama, 1259, son of the last king.
15. Bosat Wijaya Báhu, 1294, son of the last king.
16. Bhunawoka Báhu,* 1296, brother of the last king.

Of the coins of Niṣṣanka Malla and Coḍanga the Madras Museum contains no specimens, nor does it contain specimens of the copper half *massa* of Parákrama Báhu. The coinage of that monarch is, however, well represented in the museum collection by specimens of the gold Lankeṣwara; copper lion coin, of which a specimen was recently found at Kilakarai on the coast of the Madura district; copper *massa* and quarter *massa*; and a copper coin similar in every respect to the gold Lankeṣwara, found at Kilakarni, to the existence of which type no reference is made by Mr. Rhys Davids. I have also seen a specimen of the latter coin in the collection of the Rev. J. Tracy.

Following the same course as that adopted by Mr. Rhys Davids, I have placed the gold *Lakshmi*, *Tamraki* and *Iraka* coins with the Ceylon coins, though, as that authority says, "their classification is, at present, quite uncertain, and it is doubtful whether some of them belong to Ceylon at all." As regards the *Iraka* coin, which is named from the word *Iraka* (?) on the reverse, Mr. Rhys Davids suggests that the word may possibly be *Haraka* or *Daraka*. Of this coin, Captain Tufnell says :—[2] "It bears the word 'Iraha,' a Prakrit form of the Sanskrit word 'Rakshasa' (demon), above which is what may be the lotus, or possibly the conch shell of Vishnu, and it is not improbable that the Cholas of the 12th and 13th centuries were followers of that deity." Further, Sir Walter Elliot says :—[3] "Gold fanams with the Ceylon

---

[1] *On the Ancient Coins and Measures of Ceylon.* International Numismata Orientalia.
[2] *Madras Journal of Literature and Science.*
[3] *Numismata Orientalia*, 1885. Coins of Southern India, p. 133.

type on the obverse, and an indistinot Nágari reverse, are occasionally met with. I received from Tanjore two gold pieces, weighing about 8 grains. . . . . . The reverse bas three old Nágari letters, which may ho read *iraka !* or *daraka !*, throwing no light on their origin. . . . I was inclined, when I first obtained them, to assign them to the Oholas ; as they are not infrequent in the island (Ceylon) their origin is but doubtful."

I have omitted from the present catalogue, though the Madras Museum contains specimens, the large and small *sétu* bull coins, which are included by Mr. Rhys Davids in bis work. These coins, which bear on the obverse the standing figure of a Rája with a weapon (?) in his right hand, and a trisúla and sceptre in front, and on the reverse the sacred bull Nandi with the emblems of the sun and moon above, and the legend *Sétu* below, doubtless belong to Southern India, and are attributed by Sir Walter Elliot [4] to the Zamindárs of Ramnád, and Sivaganga, the office of Sétupati or guardian of Adam's bridge being one which, " though claiming a high antiquity, appears to have been conferred or restored on the Zamindár by Muttu Krishnappa Náyak, the father of Tirumala Náyak, of Madura." [5]

I have also omitted the copper coins of the Chola dynasty of the same type (called by Sir W. Elliot the Ceylon type) as the Lankeswara coin of Parákrama Báhu, bearing on the obverse the standing figure of a Rája, and on the reverse the same figure in a sitting posture with the legend *Rája Rája*. These coins, Mr. Rhys Davids says, are the coins from which he believes the whole of the Ceylon series to be derived, and they must have been introduced into Ceylon during the invasion of the island by the Oholas, prior to the time of Parákrama Báhu.

The first settlement of Europeans, the Portuguese, in Ceylon took place in 1517, in which year Albergaria obtained permission from the King of Kotta, whose territory closely adjoined Colombo, to build a factory on the latter spot for purposes of trade.

Concerning the arrival of the Portuguese off Colombo, Davy says : [6] " The natives, who first saw them, went to Cotta and informed the king that a new people was arrived, white and beautifully made, who wore iron coats and iron caps, and drank blood and ate stones ; who gave a gold coin for a fish or even a lime ; and who had a kind of instrument that could produce thunder and lightning ; and balls which, put into these instruments, would fly many miles, break ramparts, and destroy forts."

"The appearance," says Tennent, [7] " of the Portuguese in Ceylon at this critical period, served not only to check the career of the Moors, but to extinguish the independence of the native princes ; and, looking to the facility with which the former had previously superseded the Malabars, and were fast acquiring an ascendancy over the Cinghalese chiefs, it is not an unreasonable conjecture that, but for this timely appearance of a christian power in the island, Ceylon, instead of a

---

[4] Op. cit., p. 134.　　　　　　　　[5] Sir W. Elliot, op. cit., p. 134.
[6] *Account of the Interior of Ceylon and of its Inhabitants, with Travels in that Island,* 1821.
[7] *Ceylon,* vol. I, p. 633, 1860.

possession of the British crown, might, at the present day, be a Mahometan kingdom, under the rule of some Arabian adventurer." The occupation by the Portuguese was, however, the cause of constant dissension with the natives, and eventually an alliance was formed between the native princes and the Dutch to expel the Portuguese, the conditions of the treaty being made by Rajah Singha, who afterwards became sole king of the interior, on board one of the Dutch ships off Batticoloa.

In·his work on Ceylon[*] Bertolocci says:—" Whatever was the currency of Ceylon during the government of the Portuguese, no vestige now remains of it ; and an investigation of that subject could throw no light upon its present condition." On this point Mr. Rhys Davids says :—" No coins are known to have been struck by the Portuguese in or for Ceylon. Knox says that of three sorts of coin in use one was coined by the Portugals ; the king's arms on one side and the image of a friar on the other, and by the Chingulays called tangom massa. The value of one is nine-pence English ; poddi tangom, or the small tangom, is half as much ; but these were probably struck in Portugal, and not for use in Ceylon."

The last stronghold of the Portuguese in Ceylon, Jaffna, was given up in 1658, and the Dutch occupation continued till 1796, in which year the island was ceded to the English. So far back as 1763 an embassy had been despatched by the Governor of Madras to propose a treaty to Kirti Sri, the king of Kandy, but no immediate result followed. Twenty years later Trincomallee was occupied by a British force under Sir Hector Munro, but the fort was surprised by a French fleet, and the British garrison transported to Madras. In 1795 an expedition, commanded by Colonel Stuart, landed at Trincomallee, which capitulated in three weeks. Later in the same year Calpentyn was occupied, and early in 1796 Negombo and Colombo were taken possession of, and a convention was signed, by which Point de Galle, Matura, and the remaining fortified places were ceded to Great Britain.

During the Dutch occupation large numbers of the coins of the Dutch East India Company, many bearing the monogram, v.o.o. found their way to the island, but these I shall deal with on a future occasion. As regards the European coins, which were struck specially for Ceylon, I cannot do better than quote in detail the observations of Mr. Rhys Davids, who says :—" The Dutch struck only a very few silver rix dollars, which are very rare, if not entirely extinct, and which I have never seen. A thick copper *stuiver* having on the obverse the monogram, v.o.c., the o and c written over the sides of the v, and in the open part of the v the letter c, perhaps for Colombo or Ceylon, is occasionally met with. On the reverse is the legend 1 *stuiver*, the numeral 1 being above the word *stuiver* (which occupies the centre of the field coin), and having four dots on each side of it. Below is the date, the dates in my collection being 1784, 1785, 1786, 1789, 1791, 1793, 1795. It is possible, however, that this c is only a mint mark, and that these coins, whose rough execution shows them to have been struck in the Dutch East Indies (the monogram, v.o.c., stands for the

* *View of the Agricultural, Commercial, and Financial Interests of Ceylon*, 1817.

initial letters of Vereinigte Ostindische Compagnie, *i.e.*, United East India Company) were not, after all, struck in Ceylon. There are similar coins with two apparently Tamil letters below the words stuiver, and with T and o in the place of c. If these letters stand for Trinkomalei and Galle, then one would expect Cinghalese letters, but they look like the Tamil letters I. L. for Ilankei, the Tamil form of Lanká, that is, Ceylon.

"The English have issued four types of coins besides the present ·one. Type 1, which is thick and coarsely executed, has on the ohverse an elephant, below which is the date ; on the reverse the words CEYLON GOVERNMENT round a circle, within which is the value of the coin. Of this type there are three thick silver pieces (very rare) of the value of 96, 48, and 24 stuivers (4 of which = 1 fanam), weighing 280, 140, and 70 grains, respectively. The 48 stuiver piece is equal to the rix dollar, and the three thick copper pieces of this type are, respectively, worth $\frac{1}{12}$, $\frac{1}{24}$, and $\frac{1}{48}$, of its value. These copper coins weigh 50 stuivers to the pound, and are now difficult to procure.

"Of this type, specimens of the following years, without letters, are in my collection, and those of the years marked (B.M.), are added from the British museum collection :—

Silver, 96 Stuivers, 1808 (B.M.), 1809 (B.M.).
,, 48 ,, 1803 (B.M.), 1804 (B.M.), 1808, 1809 (B.M.).
,, 24 ,, 1803, 1804 (D.M.), 1808 (B.M.).
Copper, 4 ,, 1803 (B.M.), 1804, 1805 (B.M.), 1811 (B.M.), 1814, 1815.
,, 2 ,, 1801, 1802, 1803, 1805 (B.M.), 1811, 1812 (B.M.), 1813 (B.M.), 1814, 1815, 1816.
,, 1 ,, 1801, 1802, 1803 (B.M.), 1809, 1811 (B.M.), 1812, 1813, 1814, 1815, 1817.

"Of Type 2 one issue was made, in copper, in 1802, of stuivers, half stuivers, and quarter stuivers ; they are thin, like modern coins, and well executed, weighing 36 stuivers to 1 lh., obverse and reverse as on the last type. The British museum has specimens of this type, dated 1804, but it is not certain whether they were ever in circulation. .

"Of type 3 also one issue was made, in 1815, of two-stuiver, stuiver, and half stuiver pieces in copper, and one issue of rix dollars in silver in 1821. Obverse of the copper, head of George III to right, with legend GEORGIUS. III. D.G. BRITANNIARUM. REX.: of the silver, head of Geo. IV. to left, with legend GEORGIUS. IV. D.G. BRITANNIARUM. REX. F.D. Reverse of the copper, an elephant to left ; above the legend, *Ceylon two stivers, one stiver,* or *one-half stiver,* with the date below. The silver the same, but the legend is *Ceylon one rix dollar,* and round the elephant a wreath of flowers. The coins of this type are still occasionally met with in the hazárs, but the half staiver is very difficult to get. Both this and the last issue were struck in England.

"Lastly, fanam pieces of two kinds were struck in silver. The first, which is very rare, and was issued about 1820, has simply round a small circle with a dot in its centre PANAM on one side and TOKEN on the other of a silver coin less than $\frac{2}{5}$ of an inch in diameter, and without date. The work-people, who built Baddegama church, the oldest English church in Ceylon, are said to have been paid in this coin, which is roughly executed. The other, which is half an inch in diameter, has on the obverse the bust of Victoria surrounded by the legend VICTORIA. D.G. BRITANNIAR. REGINA. F.D. and on the reverse the figures 1½ and the date 1842, surmounted by a crown and surrounded by a wreath. This little coin, seldom met with in Ceylon, is beautifully executed, and was struck in England; whilst the *fanam tokens* were struck in Ceylon.

"There is, in the British Museum, one silver specimen of another type, but whether this is a proof of an unpublished coin, or a specimen of a coin in actual circulation, I have been unable to ascertain. It has on the obverse the words TWO RIX DOLLARS in a square tablet surmounted by a crown; above it, Ceylon; below it on a scroll, DIEU ET MON DROIT, and below that again the word CURRENCY; on the reverse an elephant to the left, and below it the date 1812."

As regards the little coin mentioned above, with the figures 1½ and the date 1842, Captain Tufnell says: [*] "The description so exactly corresponds with that of the 1½d. of the 'Maunday' money, that I cannot but think that the specimens alluded to belong to that series, or to an issue of this silver piece, still to a certain extent in circulation in Malta as a fraction of 3d, which sum appears to be the most usual charge for all small commodities and services in Valetta."

---

[*] *Madras Journ. Lit. and Science*, 1838, p. 187.

CATALOGUE

OF

CEYLON COINS IN THE MADRAS MUSEUM.

No.	Metal.	Obv.	Rev.
		PARÁKRAMA BÁHU.	
		1153–1186 A.D.	
		LANKEŞWARA GOLD COIN.	
1	An.	Standing figure r; dhoti in folds on each side of, and between the legs; conical hat on head; in the r. hand a weapon, and to l. of this a sceptre (?); in l. hand a lotus flower. The figure stands on a snake with a small hole in the centre. To l. below l. arm are five dots, and a lotus flower.	The same figure as on the obverse seated, and holding lotus flower in l. hand; a grating below l. leg on the l. side of the figure inscription Ṣrī. Lankeşwara.
2	,,	,,	,,
		LANKEŞWARA COPPER COIN.	
3	Ae.	,,	,,
		COPPER MASSA.	
4	,,	Standing figure holding weapon in r. hand; below to r. lotus flower and five dots.	Seated figure and inscription. Ṣrī. Parákrama Báhu.
5	,,	,,	,,
		COPPER QUARTER MASSA.	
5·1	,,	,,	,,

No.	Metal.	Obv.	Rev.
		COPPER LION COIN.	
6	Ae.	Standing figure holding weapon in r. hand, and lotus flower in l. A lion sitting r. with mouth open, and exposing the teeth in the upper jaw.	Seated figure and inscription *Sri. Parâkrama Báhu.*
7	,,	,,	,,
		VIJAYA BÁHU.	
		1186–1187 A.D.	
8	,,	Standing figure holding weapon in r hand; below to r. lotus flower and dots.	Seated figure and inscription *Sri. Vijaya Báhu.*
9	,,	,,	,,
		GOLD FANAM.	
9·1	Au.	,,	*Sri. Vijaya Báhu.*
		LÍLÁVATÍ.	
		1197–1200 A.D.	
10	Ae.	,,	Seated figure and inscription *Sri. Rája Lílávati.*
		SÁHASA MALLA.	
		1200–1202 A.D.	
11	,,	Standing figure holding weapon in r hand; below to r. lotus flower and dots.	Seated figure and inscription *Sri. Mat. Sáhasa. Malla.*
12	,,	,,	,,
		DHARMÁSOKA.	
		1208–1209 A.D.	
13	,,	Standing figure holding weapon in r. hand; below to r. lotus flower and dots.	Seated figure and inscription *Sri. Dharmmásoka Deva.*

No.	Metal.	Obv.	Rev.

BHUVANAIKA BÁHU.

1296 A.D.

14	Ae.	Standing figure holding weapon in r. hand; below to r. lotus flower and dots.	Seated figure and inscription *Sri. Bhuvanaika Báhu.*

GOLD LAKSHMÍ COIN.

15	Au.	Standing figure, with ornament above r. arm, and trident below l. arm.	Inscription *Lakshmí* with symbol of lotus (?) above.

GOLD TAMRAKÍ COIN.

15·1	,,	,,	Inscription *Tamrakí* with symbol of lotus (?) above.

GOLD IRAKA COIN.

16	,,	Standing figure with weapon in r. hand, and lotus flower in l.; trident below l. arm.	Inscription *Iraka* (?) with symbol of lotus flower (?) and a stroke and dot above.
17	,,	,,	,,
18	,,	,,	The same inscription, with a circle and two dots above.

SILVER HOOK MONEY.[1]

19	Ar.	Bar of silver bent into a hook, with a mark stamped upon it.	

SILVER LANKA MONEY.

20	,,	Bar of silver bent so as to be slipped into the belt, with an Arabic inscription on both sides.	

DUTCH 1789.

20·1	Ae.	v.o.o. with the letter o. in open part of the v, and s.T. below.	Date 1789, and legend ම ව (IL).[2]

[1] For note on this money *see* Rhys Davids op. cit., pp. 33–35.
[2] " For Ilankei, the Tamil form of Lanka, *i.e.*, Ceylon" Rhys Davids.

No.	Metal.	Obv.	Rev.
		EUROPEAN COINAGE.	
		DUTCH 1 90.	
21	Ae.	v.o.c. with the letter T. in open part of the v.	I ST. 1790.
		DUTCH 1795.	
22	,,	v.o.c., with the letter o. in open part of the v.	I STUIVER, 1795.
22·1	,,	,,	,,
		BRITISH.	
23	,,	CEYLON GOVERNMENT round a circle, within which is the number 12.	Elephant l. with 1801 below.
24	,,	CEYLON GOVERNMENT round a circle, within which is the number 48.	Elephant l. with 1802 below.
25	,,	,,	,,
26	,,	,, but 96.	,,
27	,,	,, but 192.	,,
27·1	,,	,, but 48.	,, but 1803.
28	Ar.	CEYLON GOVERNMENT round a circle, within which is the value of the coin 24 ST.	Elephant l. with 1805 below.
29	,,	,, but 48 ST.	,, but 1808.
30	,,	Same as No. 28.	,, but 1809.
30·1	,,	,,	Elephant r. with 1811 below.
31	,,	CEYLON GOVERNMENT round a circle, within which is the number 24.	Elephant l. with 1815 below.
32	,,	,,	,,
33	,,	GEORGIUS III. D. G. BRITANNIARUM REX. Bust of the king r.	Elephant l. with inscription CEYLON TWO STIVERS above, and 1815 below.

No.	Metal.	Obv.	Rev.
		EUROPEAN COINAGE—*continued*.	
34	Ae.	GEORGIUS III. D. G. BRITAN-NIARUM REX. Bust of the king r.	Elephant l. with inscription CEYLON TWO STIVERS above, and 1815 below.
35	,,	,,	,, but ONE STIVER.
36	,,	,,	,, but HALF STIVER.
		SILVER FANAM TOKEN.	
37	Ar.	FANAM round a circle with a dot in centre.	TOKEN round a circle with a dot in centre.
38	,,	,,	,,
		SILVER RIX DOLLAR.	
39	,,	GEORGIUS IV D. G. BRITAN-NIAR. REX. Bust of the king l.	Elephant l. with CEYLON ONE RIX DOLLAR above, floral wreath and date 1821 below.
40	Ae.	VICTORIA QUEEN. Bust of the queen l.	CEYLON FIVE CENTS 1870 round a circle, within which is a palm tree, and the value of the coin—5 cents—in Tamil and Cinghalese.
41	,,	,,	,,
42	,,	,,	CEYLON ONE CENT 1870 round a circle, within which is a palm tree, and the value of the coin—1 cent—in Tamil and Cinghalese.
43	,,	,,	,,
44	,,	,,	CEYLON HALF CENT 1870 round a circle, within which is a palm tree, and the value of the coin—$\frac{1}{2}$ cent—in Tamil and Cinghalese.
45	,,	,,	CEYLON QUARTER CENT 1870 round a circle, within which is a palm tree, and the value of the coin—$\frac{1}{4}$ cent—in Tamil and Cinghalese.

No.	Metal.	Obv.	Rev.
		EUROPEAN COINAGE—*continued.*	
46	Ar.	VICTORIA D.G. BRITANNIAB. REGINA. F. D. Bust of the queen l.	HALF FARTHING with crown above and 1843 and rose, shamrock, and thistle below.
47	,,	,,	,,
48	,,	Defaced.	,, but QUARTER FARTHING. 1853.
49	,,	,,	,,
50	,,	VICTORIA QUEEN. Bust of the queen l.	CEYLON. 50 CENTS. 1892. Palm tree, and value of the coin in Tamil and Cinghalese.
51	,,	,,	,, but 1893.
52	,,	,,	CEYLON. 25 CENTS 1892. Palm tree, and value of the coin in Tamil and Cinghalese.
53	,,	,,	,, but 1893.
54	,,	,,	CEYLON. 10 CENTS 1892. Palm tree, and value of the coin in Tamil and Cinghalese.
55	,,	,,	,, but 1893.
		TOKEN.	
56	,,	TATHAM & CO. COLOMBO CEYLON.	SVDDUWELLE MILLS.
57	,,	,,	,,